A Delightful Romp Through Regency England. . .

Something Wild

Lady Madeline's first and only London season lasts one month before a family emergency forces her home. The memory of one gentleman remains with her, in particular his face and eyes.

Six years later Lady Madeline has the keeping of her sister's four children. She approaches Lord Baylor, a neighbor, to ask a favor, but with Lord Baylor is the gentleman she remembers from her one, short season; he is now the Earl of Spode. Her wild nature is intrigued.

Robert, the Earl of Spode, immediately recognizes Lady Madeline. She was the lovely young girl with the eyes—big, beautiful green eyes. He hopes to get close to Lady Madeline —and make sure she doesn't disappear from his life again.

Sweet Sauerkraut

Nick, Viscount Wharncliffe, has sold his commission so he can raise his five nephews—hellions all. Deciding he needs a wife, he comes to London where he meets a fellow officer. Major Reese tells Nick he has a sister who loves to cook, and comes with a substantial dowry.

Nick knows this is his prayer answered. He'll woo the girl and wed her with her brother's blessing. She can cook her heart away and fill the bottomless pits of the five little monsters while he uses part of her dowry to continue repairs to the house.

What Nick doesn't count on is falling in love with Beth. His conscience won't allow him to offer for her—the five little beasts would surely see her to an early grave.

Joy's Christmas Wishes

Eleven-year-old Joy wishes her father to marry Lady Emily so he'll remain at home instead of leaving her and her three brothers months at a time while he captains his ship.

Captain Geoffrey DeBohun never intends to give up the sea. Nor does he look to remarry. But when he feels his blood thrum when close to Lady Emily—as it used to do with his first wife—he decides to pursue this woman.

Lady Emily doesn't want to be drawn to Captain Geoffrey DeBohun. She believes her brother, the Earl of Spode, has Geoffrey DeBohun's brother in mind for her, the Earl of Wickerdun. When Joy's first wish comes true, Emily wonders if perhaps the girl might get her Christmas wishes after all.

The Passage To Summer

When the normally formal and proper Earl of Wickerdun enters an enchanted forest, his world turns upside down. Songs from wood nymphs, and an aqua-eyed faery make him think he's on his way to Bedlam, yet he never felt so alive. Is she mortal or has she truly enchanted him?

Only and Always You

Ten years ago, two hearts were broken. Will Viscount Seton and Lady Claire be able to set aside their hurt and betrayal to have a second chance at love with each other?

A Chorus Singing Love

Lady Melody Bruin knows Trevor Wilde, the Earl of Ardmoor, is the other half of her soul. Due to The Unfortunate Incident of the summer of 1807, Ardmoor wants nothing to do with her. When an invitation arrives for Melody to spend the Christmas Holiday with the Earl and Countess of Spode, Melody knows this is her last chance to win Ardmoor's heart.

On the

Wild Side

Gerri Bowen

A Regency Romance Anthology

On the Wild Side

An Original Publication of
Highland Press Publishing - 2009

Cover by Deborah MacGillivray and Monika Wolmarans

For information, please contact
Highland Press Publishing,
PO Box 2292, High Springs, FL 32655.
www.highlandpress.org

ISBN - 978-0-9842499-1-6

PUBLISHED BY HIGHLAND PRESS PUBLISHING

A Wee Dram Book

"I love you not only for what you are,
but for what I am when I am with you."

~Elizabeth Barrett Browning

Contents

Something Wild

Chapter One
Lady Madeline Marches Forth, Seeking Aid

Madeline tied the ribbons of her black bonnet securely under her chin, carefully buttoned her gloves, adjusted her shawl just so and then studied her reflection in the mirror. A very proper looking woman stared back. With a satisfied nod she called for her nephews.

When Larkwing, their butler, appeared, she informed him she and the twins would be visiting Highspot.

"I don't expect to be long. But if my brother should awaken and ask for me . . ."

Larkwing nodded and held the door. Madeline grabbed her twin nephews by their collars as they dashed past.

"We will walk briskly, not run," she told them. "You will escort me and offer your arms, if you please." She nodded when their arms were linked. "You are ten and four, therefore no jumping in puddles. Nor *walking* through puddles. I wish to arrive at Highspot in as immaculate a state as possible, if you please."

"Do you think Lord Baylor will help?" Simon asked.

"That is what I hope to determine. Which is why you both must be on your best behavior whilst I'm inside." She gave her severe look to each in turn. "No sneaking up on grooms or servants, no screams, nor behind-closed-door noises. Not only is my future in peril, but yours as well if Sir Insufferable the toad-face, shite-breath, chinless scoundrel has his way." She blinked rapidly. "Ignore what I just said." She shook her head. *Her wildness was escaping again.*

"Why doesn't Uncle Trevor deal with Sir Insufferable?" Hunter asked. "He's a hero."

Madeline harrumphed. "My brother has yet to reconcile himself to the fact that, although he returned home alive, he returned home minus a leg."

"Half a leg," Hunter corrected. "Well, gone from below the knee. About—"

"Since I've had the care of my brother, I *know* how much of his leg remains."

"She meant metaphorically, dolt, not literally," Simon said.

"You're the dolt!"

Madeline halted, perforce bringing her nephews to a halt. "We will not engage in fighting, verbally or figuratively, *if you please.*"

"He's a hero," Hunter muttered once they resumed walking. "Doesn't matter if most of his leg is gone."

Madeline nodded once. "A hero and well-respected officer. Unfortunately, so lost in self-pity he doesn't realize his life hasn't ended. Merely changed."

Hunter grinned at his aunt. "*I* would never stay abed all day and drink brandy. *I* would learn how to ride again, and help—"

Simon stopped. "You can't know that! Our uncle was a hero, an officer, and now he's nothing! How would you feel if all you knew was taken from you?"

Madeline's eyes brimmed over. Whether from Simon's surprisingly compassionate speech, or the fact his words echoed her fears, she didn't know.

"He is too something! He's the Earl of Ardmoor!"

The twins stood nose to nose.

"Well . . ." Madeline could see Simon strived for a retort. "His own brother had to die for him to become earl!"

She lifted her chin. "Enough of this, if you please!"

* * * *

Simon and Hunter remained where their aunt left them for perhaps all of two minutes. Then they wandered about the circled drive, kicking at the gravel.

"What if Lord Baylor doesn't help?" Simon asked. "Or believes, as the vicar does, she should wed Sir Insufferable?"

"She was nervous," Hunter said. "She always walks fast when she's nervous."

"And says, 'if you please' as if it *didn't* please her to say so."

They looked back at the house. "I wish we could do something," Simon said.

"I think our idea of using the longbow on Sir Insufferable worth pursuing."

Simon shook his head. "We might kill him. Our aim isn't as good as hers."

"If *father* were here—"

"He's not, and we never know when he'll put back in." Simon frowned. "There must be something we could do. Once father returns he said we'd be old enough to join him on ship."

"What about Henry and Joy? Aunt Maddy would still have them."

"Henry's only twelve, so that's two years before she'd have to worry about that silly longbow law. Joy's a girl, so it doesn't apply to her."

"Aunt Maddy should get herself a husband."

Simon snorted. "*That's* what started this debacle."

"How come you know so many more words than I do?"

"I'm the eldest."

Hunter rolled his eyes. "By minutes."

* * * *

Madeline's stomach plummeted when her planned audience with Lord Baylor was postponed. Lady Baylor came upon her and insisted she greet their guests, going so far as to link her arm through Madeline's arm so Madeline couldn't escape.

She cringed. She would have avoided Highspot if she'd known the baron and his wife had returned with guests. Now her requested audience would have to wait. Even worse, she would have to pay particular attention to what she said. And how she behaved. Did other women have this problem? *Only wild women*, a little voice inside answered. Madeline wanted to jump up and down on that little voice.

There were two couples inside the drawing room with Baron Baylor. All looked with interest when she and Lady Baylor entered. Madeline heard Lady Baylor's laughter, heard her say something witty about finding her in the hall. Madeline supposed it was witty; her mind ceased to function as soon as she had seen *him*. People laughed. *He* laughed. Then began the introductions. Madeline could feel her heart beat faster. It was *him!* The gentleman from her short season. He was an earl? The Earl of Spode? She didn't think he was an earl six years ago.

"I remember Lady Madeline," he said as he smiled and bowed over her gloved hand.

What was she to say to that? I remember you as well? Yours is the only face I recall from my short, happy season? His dark hair had a mahogany tint and a bit of curl. She pulled her gaze from the intriguing implications of his hair, and focused on his eyes. Ah, yes. His eyes were a dark amber in color, edged with thick lashes. Many a night she'd sighed over the memory of those eyes; what might have developed between them had she remained in London.

His voice was low. "I regret we never shared the supper dance you promised me," he said.

Ah, but you have no idea how much I have regretted that as well. Madeline smiled and said nothing. Did he really remember her? The others were introduced. Lady Emily was his sister. Baron Whiteleaf and Lady Diana were brother and sister. How many minutes must pass before she could excuse herself? She couldn't help but look in the earl's direction. Which caused a blush to rise because he always met her stare.

"Are you related to the new Earl of Ardmoor, Lady Madeline?" Baron Whiteleaf asked.

"My brother."

"Ah. Yet isn't the principal holding in Surrey?"

Madeline inclined her head. "I prefer Cornwall."

"Is your brother with you? I believe he was wounded at Orthez?"

"Yes."

"You were in London, Lady Madeline?" Lady Diana asked. "Some years ago, I presume?"

Madeline looked at Lady Diana. Although grateful for the change in topic, she didn't care for the way Lady Diana eyed her outdated clothes. "Six years ago, yes." Madeline smiled.

Lady Diana leaned forward. "The *ton* can be cruel when one doesn't take."

"I'm sorry, Lady Diana, I wouldn't know. I took. My season was cut short."

Lady Diana drew back and narrowed her eyes. "You are in mourning?"

"Lady Madeline," Lady Baylor said as she gave Madeline a sharp look, "should be out of her mourning, but refuses to don color."

"Yes," Madeline agreed. How to explain she used her black and grey clothes as a defense against unwanted attention?

All looked up when the doors opened. Madeline rose. "Such a lovely visit, but we—"

"Nonsense. Stay where you are," Lady Baylor said. With a large smile she ushered the twins inside.

"Sorry," Simon said, though he didn't look the least bit sorry.

"It was beginning to rain," Hunter said. "Is there tea?"

* * * *

Robert Baideson, the twelfth Earl of Spode, gave silent thanks to whom or whatever had brought Lady Madeline back into his life. She was as lovely as he remembered. More so. Well, what he saw of her. Her bonnet covered her hair, but he assumed it was still red; a pretty sort of red streaked with gold. Her figure impossible to determine due to the shapeless gown and drab shawl she wore. The girl he recalled had a figure that showed promise of developing into something a man might never tire of loving. That he would have to determine. Robert remembered her eyes in particular. Large eyes a shade of green that brought to mind deep woods and moss and wood nymphs, and dappled sunshine on naked, white skin.

Robert was content for the nonce to watch and listen. He believed he'd found his countess, but six years had passed, after all. She might have changed, but he didn't believe so. She'd recognized him when they were introduced. There had been awareness when he'd looked into her eyes; her fingers had trembled in his; her lips had parted, as if in invitation. That certain something had been present when they touched—six years ago and again just minutes ago. Now he'd found her, and if she proved to be all he thought, he would woo her.

Robert was not pleased by Lady Diana's questions, but admired Lady Madeline's refusal to be insulted; she showed herself to good advantage. But he could tell his future countess was uncomfortable by the questions asked by Whiteleaf. A poser. Why should such questions make her uncomfortable?

When her nephews entered the room, Robert thought she might swoon. But his future countess was made of sterner stuff than that. She gave them each a look, promising severe retribution—though he was pleased to note she managed such a feat with none but he the wiser. Although one might argue the boys too young to participate in afternoon tea with adults, Robert was impressed by their maturity. Lord, he remembered himself at that age. Her nephews conduct and conversation were exemplary. As it appeared Lady Madeline had their raising for the past six years . . . his future countess acquitted herself well on that score.

Robert's attention focused on the conversation when he saw Lady Madeline's lips press together. Saw her ram-rod back inch higher; he wouldn't have thought that possible. Whiteleaf had said something to the boys about ships. When he saw her rise, he stood, and pulled up his sister as well.

"Emily and I will be pleased to accompany you and your nephews, Lady Madeline."

His sister turned to him in question. He looked at her, trying to convey with his eyes what he couldn't say aloud. *Do this or surrender your allowance for the next century.*

"Wait until I get my bonnet," Emily said, and gracefully exited the drawing room.

* * * *

Robert learned a great deal from the twins on their walk home. Some of which was useful to him. Most important, he learned the reason for Lady Madeline's visit to Highspot.

"I've heard of sillier laws," Robert said to the twins. Lady Madeline and his sister walked ahead, and he enjoyed watching the sway of his future countess' hips, but the presence of her nephews precluded more acute observation. "I shouldn't think it too difficult to change the law; I could introduce legislation. Or find a more sympathetic clergyman, for that matter. You say the way the law is now, all males over the age of fourteen must practice the longbow two hours a week under the supervision of a clergyman?"

"Local clergyman," Simon said.

"And your vicar refuses?"

"That's why our aunt wanted to talk to Lord Baylor, to see if he could talk to the vicar, or talk to Sir Insuf—Sir Basil," Hunter said.

"Why does Sir Basil pursue this? To my knowledge our country no longer depends on bowmen for her defense."

"Aunt Madeline says it is his way to plague her into accepting him as husband."

Robert pursed his lips and glanced at Simon. "Does your aunt pine for another? Is that why she is unwed?" He wondered at the glance the twins exchanged.

"She says she has enough just with the four of us." Hunter smiled at him. "But we'll be going with our father when he sets sail again. He captains his own ship! Only Henry and Joy will be here, and then soon they'll be gone. Our aunt won't have anyone."

"She'll have Ardmoor, our uncle. But I expect he'll marry and then our Aunt Maddy will be all alone." Simon sighed loudly.

Robert nodded. "No doubt it would ease your mind to know your aunt happily wed."

He saw them look at one another as if to say they hadn't thought it would be so easy. Robert smiled. "I think I should tell you . . ."

* * * *

Emily didn't want to walk with Lady Madeline, for she thought the woman cold, more concerned with propriety than conversation. But as it was obvious her brother had developed an unaccountable *interest* in the woman, Emily would oblige his request. As their walk progressed, Emily changed her mind. Lady Madeline was all that was pleasant, pointing out flowers and shrubs, birds familiar to Cornwall, even speaking of local legends and myths. She asked Emily about her season, and told amusing stories of her own, short season. They conversed amiably until they reached Ardmoor House, where both seemed loath to end their speech.

Lady Madeline invited them in, but her brother declined, and instead asked if they might visit on the morrow.

When it looked to Emily as if her new friend was unsure whether or not to agree, her brother said he thought he might have a plan to thwart Sir Insufferable. Might he speak further on the subject when he and his sister visited on the morrow?

Emily saw Lady Madeline's face turn red. But then Lady Madeline burst out in laughter, as did everyone else.

Lady Madeline's eyes still held laughter when she spoke. "Very well, Lord Spode. I look forward to seeing you both."

* * * *

"I thought her cold in the beginning," Emily said as they walked back to Highspot, "but she is not; merely reserved, let us say. Her fire is hidden. I like her."

"Good. I intend to make her my countess." He smiled when Emily turned to him in surprise. "What? You said you liked her."

"I do! But . . . but isn't this sudden? You would wed her after an afternoon's acquaintance?"

He shook his head. "That would be foolish, indeed. No, Em, I've wondered about her for six years. Though she was one of many, she stood out from all the other debutantes six years ago. It took me weeks to get up my courage to speak to her. When I did, I asked her for a dance for the next evening's ball. But it was too late. She was called home and I never saw her again."

"Oh!" Emily held her hands to her chest. "That is so romantic."

"Romantic? No, it was foolish of me to waste all those days and weeks."

"But think, had she remained, you might even now be wed."

Robert shook his head. "Remember, I was the third son six years ago. She an earl's daughter. Her family would never have countenanced the alliance."

"But now," Emily said with a smile, "now you and she—"

"I have to woo her, Em. She's no young miss with thoughts only to snare a husband. Six years she's had the raising of her three nephews and niece, making them a home, and she's done well. She might not want to wed."

Emily wrinkled her nose. "Not wed you! Don't be silly."

Robert smiled. "You'll have to help me with this, Em."

Emily nodded. "Of course I shall help you. If you're sure. Lady Baylor might assist as well, for she appears fond of Lady Madeline."

"Then too, there's that silly law . . . I'm sure I can use that to my advantage."

* * * *

Madeline grabbed each twin by an ear, ignored their howls of outrage, and walked briskly into the drawing room where she released them and stood with her hands on her hips. "You will explain to me why you entered Highspot. Why you conversed about your father with Baron Whiteleaf. How Lord Spode came to call Sir Basil, Sir Insufferable. *If you please.*"

* * * *

The arrival of more guests postponed Robert's planned questioning of Lady Baylor. Not wanting to draw attention to Lady Madeline's name, he hesitated speaking to their hostess unless tête-a-tête. Lady Diana solved his dilemma by speaking of Lady Madeline later that evening. Lady Baylor took exception to Lady Diana's words and tone, and admiringly defended Lady Madeline to one and all.

Robert was pleased by what he heard. Nothing to disqualify her as his countess.

* * * *

"He thought being the third son would exclude him as a suitor?" Madeline looked from Simon to Hunter. "He spoke to you of this?"

The twins looked at one another and back to her. "We were talking," Simon said, and kicked his shoe against the carpet.

"We talked about many things," Hunter said. "He said *his* father didn't object when one of his brothers went into trade. Well, it was the East India Company."

"You talked about that?" Madeline sat and fanned her face. "You know not to draw attention to yourselves. You *know* your father's family is looking for you." She put her hands to cool her cheeks. "I despise that silly law. If not for that law and Sir Basil—"

"We didn't tell him who our father is," Simon said.

"We're not *dolts*," Hunter said.

Simon put a hand on her shoulder. "He said he could help."

Hunter put his hand on her other shoulder. "We like him, Aunt Maddy. He talked to us like we were adults."

"We think you should allow him to help. What could it hurt?"

Madeline closed her eyes and pictured Lord Robert Baideson, Earl of Spode. With her fingers running through his hair. Even worse, she could picture herself on his lap, pulling his head back so she could kiss him. Where did such thoughts come from? *Your wild nature*, a little voice replied.

"Wild nature to the devil!" she cried as she rose. She looked at her nephews, aware she had spoken aloud. "Ignore what I just said."

Chapter Two
The Earl of Spode Makes His Move

Lady Baylor told Robert to avail himself of the Baylor carriage when he and his sister visited Ardmoor House, remarking not everyone enjoyed Lady Madeline's enthusiasm for long walks. Sitting in the carriage, Robert brooded over what his sister had just informed him.

"I can't think why Lady Diana should say I was set to offer for her. She may have been in the back of my mind—along with many others—but had I any firm thoughts in that direction, her manner of speech to Lady Madeline yesterday clearly showed her in an unfavorable light."

"I told Lady Baylor I thought Lady Diana was speaking more from hope; that you had never indicated your affections were with her." Emily smiled. "I did say I thought you hoped to renew your acquaintance with Lady Madeline. And if your affections were to be engaged, one should look in that direction. Lady Baylor was pleased."

"Good." Robert smiled. "You will look for my signal?"

Emily frowned. "Yes. I'll count to five hundred, but that's all the time alone you will have! I cannot in good conscience leave you alone any longer."

* * * *

Madeline thought the grey of her gown washed out any color from her complexion. It was also baggy. She tied the white cap under her chin and looked at herself. Perfectly horrid.

What would it hurt to keep off the cap? Wear a pretty gown? He wants to help you, not ravish you. Madeline sighed. The trouble was, she thought her wild nature might *want* him to ravish her. Well, not ravish—she wasn't clear on what that was exactly, but knew it must be avoided. Certainly she wanted him to kiss her. And her kiss him. She could feel her wild nature rising up and embracing all those thoughts of kissing. What *would* it hurt to have him look at her in admiration? She removed her cap and studied her head. Her braids were coiled neatly at her nape. There, that would do. She hated the cap, after all.

* * * *

Simon and Hunter were on their knees before Joy, their ten-year old sister. "Just don't mention Aunt Maddy's wild side. Anyone's wild side. Please?" Simon asked.

"We want him to marry her, Joy. Don't you want Aunt Maddy to marry?"

"No. I don't like Spodes," Joy said. "I don't want to move away. I want to stay here."

"But if Aunt Maddy married Lord Spode, they might take you to London," Simon said. "Think of all you'll see. The animals at the Tower Zoo, the shops." He looked at Hunter.

"They have everything in London," Hunter said. "Dolls! They have about a thousand doll shops in London." Hunter grinned at Simon.

Joy looked at her brothers with narrowed eyes. "They do not."

"We're begging you, Joy," Simon said. "Don't say anything to scare Lord Spode away, or Aunt Maddy might have to marry Sir Insufferable. Then Father's family might take us away. But if Aunt Maddy marries Lord Spode, he's powerful enough to protect us until Father returns home."

Joy stuck out her lower lip. "Why can't Papa come home and stay?"

Robert shifted unobtrusively in his chair—again—and steered the conversation from polite small talk to the problem at hand. Anything to keep Lady Madeline's eyes off of him, since he had the oddest notion she was mentally ravishing him. Not that he minded, but since they weren't alone, nor betrothed, he couldn't do anything about it, could he? Most disconcerting.

"I can introduce legislation to have the law changed." His eyes followed the movement of her bottom lip as she brought it between her teeth. "Or I could ask Lord Baylor to urge the vicar to do his duty." More biting. He shifted yet again. "I could speak to Sir Insufferable and declare his suit is unwanted." Her lips opened and her tongue made a brief, wet appearance. He groaned, imagining where on his body he would like those lips and tongue. "Or you could marry me." *Zounds! Had he just blurted out his proposal of marriage?*

Lady Madeline stared at him, her eyes wide, her mouth open in surprise. He hoped it was surprise and not distaste.

"Oh, that would be lovely!" Emily cried, hopping twice in her chair. "Do say yes! Ignore my brother's impetuous, ignominious proposal and say yes!"

Lady Madeline blinked. "I wouldn't say it was an ignominious proposal."

Emily laughed and clasped her hands together. "You do say yes?"

Lady Madeline shook her head and looked between him and his sister. "I can't . . . the children . . . I gave my word."

Robert arched a brow. Well. She appeared to have some reservations about becoming his countess. "I apologize for blurting out in public what should have been done privately." He frowned. "If you would accompany—"

"Robert," Emily broke in. "Shouldn't you first speak to Ardmoor? I'm aware Lady Madeline is of age, but there are proprieties to observe."

Robert wondered what his sister was about. By her expression, he could see she wanted him out of the room. No doubt to exchange words female to female. And he'd be a fool to object. "Indeed, Em, you have the right of it. Lady Madeline? If I may speak to Ardmoor?"

"Oh, but my brother . . ." Lady Madeline stopped and Robert saw her brows rise. "Yes. Yes, see him, 'tis about time Ardmoor took note of what is transpiring about in the world."

* * * *

Madeline didn't mind Lady Emily holding her hands. Nor did she object to the pleasant prospect Lady Emily made on her becoming the Countess of Spode. She appreciated Lady Emily's honesty when speaking of her brother, for although she spoke glowingly of him, she admitted he had faults and spoke of them. Madeline didn't consider being short-tempered in the morning much of a fault.

When Lady Emily spoke of how marriage to her brother would alleviate any concern over her nephews having to abide by that silly law, Madeline did admit to being tempted. In fact, she knew if she hadn't promised to keep her sister's children safe from their in-laws, she might be inclined to say yes. Madeline thought something of her thoughts must be showing in her eyes, for Lady Emily leaned closer, her smile wide, her grip almost painful.

"Do say yes! Make my brother the most happiest of men!"

* * * *

Robert stood outside Ardmoor's chamber door, where Watkins, Ardmoor's valet—although Robert would wager a year's rents it was Ardmoor's former batman—had bid him wait whilst he ascertained whether or not the earl was receiving. From where Robert stood, apparently the earl of Ardmoor was awake and bloody didn't want to bloody see any bloody, bleeding, friggin' sonofabitch he'd never heard of.

It was a tricky situation. Ardmoor a potential brother-in-law. The man obviously didn't want to see him. He couldn't barge in and demand an audience. Yet how could he return to the drawing room and admit defeat? He needed all the help he could get to win his future bride's favor. Watkins opened the door and said the earl was feeling better and would see him.

Robert entered and stated his business. That the man was still abed, his room dark and reeking of alcohol was Ardmoor's concern, not his. The man was a hero. Missing a leg, but still a hero. And now an earl.

"You want to marry Maddy?" Ardmoor lifted his arm off his face and looked at Robert. "Who are you?"

Robert repeated his name. He explained again the problem Lady Madeline was having with the silly law concerning longbow practice and Sir Insufferable. He stated his desire to wed Lady Madeline, and started to give his worth, but Ardmoor waved him off.

"She want you?"

Robert hesitated. Did she?

"She doesn't want you?"

"Possibly. I'm not sure." *Zounds, could he sound more pathetic?*

Ardmoor cursed. And took his time about it before calling for Watkins. "I expect this is a sign," he said with a loud sigh. "A sign for me to move my arse from bed."

Robert waited. *Was that a yes? A no? What did the man mean?* "I have your permission to court your sister?"

"Court her, marry her, as long as Maddy is happy." He looked up at Robert. "She tell you about the children?"

Robert knew this an important question. *What was the correct answer?* "She mentioned a promise."

Ardmoor grunted. "Wickerdun."

Robert smiled as relief filled his chest. Finally, a point of reference they could agree upon. "Wickerdun is a particular friend of mine." Robert's stomach clenched at Ardmoor's expression.

"Bloody hell. Bloody, friggin' hell. Sorry. Can't have Maddy."

"But—"

"Promises to be kept. No. My last word on the subject."

* * * *

"Who is Wickerdun to you?"

He saw Lady Madeline's welcoming smile fade, her face whiten. "Where did you hear that name?"

"Your brother." He made so bold as to grab her arm when she attempted to flee. He cast a look at his sister. "You will remain here whilst Lady Madeline and I peruse the gardens."

* * * *

Well, Lord Spode certainly knew how to kiss. Madeline drew back and studied his face with single-minded attention until she knew each bit of him. She wanted to kiss it all. And use her tongue. Lord Spode had shown her what exquisite delights could be had with using one's tongue to good advantage. She moved to kiss him again, but he held her back. Drat! He was talking again. How did he expect her to concentrate when her wild nature was running amuck?

"Just say yes, Maddy."

Maddy? When had they gone from Lady Madeline to Madeline to Maddy? "Yes?" She stepped back. "Yes to what?"

"Yes, you will marry me. Yes, you will trust me. Yes, you believe I will protect you and respect whatever promise you made concerning your nephews and niece. Yes, you will tell me why the name Wickerdun puts you in a panic."

She would have returned to the house, but he kissed her again. Only the sound of Joy's giggles reminded her where she was, and helped pull her from Lord Spode's lascivious embrace.

"Robert!" Lady Emily's voice trilled from beyond the roses.

Madeline and Lord Spode were a respectable two feet apart when his sister and her niece came into view. Madeline had to refrain from touching her lips, smoothing her hair, and straightening the bodice of her gown. She felt her eyes widen. *The bodice of her gown?*

"Robert, you *must* speak with my new little friend. Her name is Joy."

Madeline could see Lord Spode had about as much interest in talking to her niece as he had in ripping out his fingernails. But he smiled and bowed and said as how his sister had such fine taste in friends, he was delighted to meet Miss Joy. At the sight of Joy's delighted smile, Madeline's heart turned over. *He really was a fine man.*

Chapter Three
The Family Nemesis

After hearing from Ardmoor that Lord Spode was a particular friend of the Earl of Wickerdun, Madeline was all for packing up the family and heading for a distant Ardmoor estate. Ardmoor's declaration that he'd use his saber to cleave a head or two should any dare intrude upon his family's solitude made Madeline anxious to begin the journey. Then Ardmoor *would* decide to try the wooden leg Watkins had procured. And Ardmoor *would* insist on negotiating the stairs with his new peg leg. Madeline knew if she survived this day she would survive anything. Never did she expect Lord Spode to appear the next day with a man claiming to be Wickerdun.

Just as well Ardmoor decided the gardens were a more comfortable place to accustom himself to his new peg. Although his inventive curses were heard in the drawing room, his saber was stashed safely away in his locker.

Madeline narrowed her eyes at Lord Spode. The man had offered marriage only the day before. Kissed and licked her senseless. Now he appeared with the family nemesis.

"Lady Madeline, may I make known to you, William, DeBohun, the Earl of Wickerdun. William, this is Lady Madeline Wilde. The woman I hope to wed."

Madeline reluctantly curtseyed.

"It *is* good to meet you," Wickerdun said as she raised her eyes. "Can't wait to meet the nevy's and niece. Bad *ton*, bad *ton*, for m'father to cut off old Geoff. Never could see Geoff as a curate. Never understood what difference if m'brother captain's his own ship rather than join the navy. Seems to me he made the better choice. Mean to tell him that, but the man is elusive. Well," he said with a large smile, "it is good to finally meet you."

* * * *

"I am forgiven?" Robert asked after he had kissed Maddy. "Are you curious as to how I came to arrive with Wickerdun?"

"You are forgiven, and yes, I am curious."

Robert grinned. "I am a clever man, as you'll come to appreciate once we're wed." He gave her a quick kiss. "Wickerdun, as I'd told your brother, is a particular friend of mine. He was one of Lord Baylor's guests, and arrived yesterday afternoon. When I asked what he knew of the Earl of Ardmoor, he relayed the sad story of his father's casting out his younger son because he chose to captain his own ship. And the subsequent scandalous marriage—scandalous because they traveled to Gretna Green to marry—of the eldest daughter of the Ardmoor house to his brother. And his father's determination to raise his son's children as befitted the grandsons of an earl. So I, being the clever man that I am, deduced that your hiding here in Cornwall was rooted in the fear someone might recognize your nephews and take them from you. Wickerdun has no inclination to take on his brother's children. But I would be happy to share your duty. Now, you have no reason to refuse my offer of marriage."

He thought Madeline looked tempted. "My sister once warned me," she whispered, and he leaned close. "She said be careful whom I favored, for there is a wildness in our blood, a wildness not often matched in those we favor. It can prove disastrous when our . . . wildness is not returned."

"Your niece bemoaned something about the Wilde wild nature. Apparently she hopes to inveigle Emily into wedding your brother-in-law."

He saw Madeline's eyes widen and her lips part. He didn't want her to think about that, so he nuzzled her ear before whispering to her. "Tell me more of the Wilde wild nature.

Wild as in sharing the blood of . . . Shenti? Dennene? Pelldari?"

She pulled away and looked him in his eyes. "How do you come to know those names? Are you . . .?"

"I am the Earl of Spode. Don't you know your own history?"

She shook her head. "But I'm gladdened you do." His blood stirred at the sight of her smile. "That means we share the same wild blood." Her eyes roamed his face hungrily, and then she laughed.

"What is so funny?"

"That silly law. Now I'm thankful it exists."

"As it helped bring us together once again, so am I." And then he kissed her.

~~~

Great Britain • All English males over age 14
are to carry out two or so hours of longbow
practice a week supervised by the local clergy.

Sweet Sauerkraut

Chapter One
To London to Seek a Wife

"Major! Ardmoor!" Nick hailed, recognizing the man attempting to climb the steps to White's. Ardmoor's wooden leg didn't appear cooperative.

Ardmoor turned and gave a brief nod. "Bloody peg has a mind of its own." He made another attempt up the steps, this time using his walking stick to aid him.

Nick knew better than to offer assistance. "I've got your back, major." He heard a bark of laughter from Ardmoor as they made their way up.

"Surprised to see you in London," Ardmoor said when they stepped inside. "Bring the bloody monsters with you?"

"Yes." Nick ran a hand through his hair. "Couldn't find anyone to stay with them. Can't keep a cook or housekeeper. They slip away in the night, never to be seen."

"Sure the bloody beasts haven't done away with them?"

"They say they only tie them up, never harm them." He ignored Ardmoor's snort. "Decided I'd come to London and hire from here. Thought a woman wouldn't be as likely to flee if she had to travel all the way to London from Yorkshire. I'm looking for a wife as well. A woman with a large dowry." Nick met Ardmoor's grin with a scowl. "I've gone through most of the funds I'd set aside for renovating Gorse Grange. Didn't count on a new roof!"

Ardmoor grunted. "Find a wife first, a bloody rich wife. Let her do the hiring. And remember, a wife can't run. Ah, there's Reese."

Nick was pleasantly surprised to see Major Reese, now Mr. Reese since he'd sold his commission.

"Reese has called a meeting," Ardmoor said. "Something about his sister. Might as well join us."

* * * *

Nick greeted his friends, Major Reese and Captain Doune, but his thoughts remained on his immediate problem—his five nephews. No, they *were* monsters, Ardmoor had the right of it. Marry a wealthy woman. Ardmoor had the right of that as well. A wife couldn't run away. Well, she *could*. He'd have to make sure she didn't. Except he first had to find a woman, woo and wed her before she met the little beasts.

"It isn't natural!" Reese said. "The gel says she'll hire herself out." He nodded at the murmurs. "Her grandfather's an earl! It isn't done! Told her she should get herself married, fill her nursery and she'd soon forget her foolishness. Laughed at me and patted my cheek. Told me not to worry."

Nick sat forward. "Your sister likes to cook so much she'd hire herself out?"

"What's her dowry?" Ardmoor asked at the same time.

Nick watched Reese glance around before whispering to Ardmoor. At the sight of Ardmoor's raised brows, Nick's pulse quickened. Might Reese be intent on finding a husband for the chit? Lord knew, he needed a wife with a substantial dowry.

"Is she a good cook?" he asked.

Reese flushed red and leaned forward. "Better than my Fanny," he whispered and held a finger to his lips.

The men whistled softly. Everyone knew Reese's wife, who chose to follow the drum after her marriage to Major Reese, was famous for her culinary expertise. Nick had never eaten better than when dining with the Reese's. And the man thought his sister's cooking was superior to Mrs. Reese's? If they wed, the woman could cook her heart away. His nephews were bottomless pits. This began to sound like a prayer answered.

"Now that Fanny and I are home, we share the house with my father. He's happy we're there. Bit awkward with my sister still at home though, since she's been running the house for years. Besides, Fanny is . . . er . . . we're expecting an interesting event later this year."

"About bloody time," Ardmoor said. "No offense intended."

"Five years and nothing," Reese said. "Home four months and she's breeding. Told her it was that nasty brew she insisted on drinking each morning over there. Since we've been home, she said she lost her taste for it." He shrugged. "I want my Fanny happy and content. She deserves that much."

"Bloody understandable. How old's the sister?"

"Two and twenty." Reese cocked his head at Ardmoor. "Are you . . .?"

Nick's brows raised when Ardmoor shook his head and pointed to him.

"Not bloody likely! Nick. Viscount Wharncliffe. He wants a bride."

* * * *

"That wasn't so bad, now was it?" Reese patted his sister's arm as he looked around the ballroom for a familiar face.
They'd made it through the receiving line. Thank God. Ardmoor had been standing next to his sister and her husband, the Earl and Countess of Spode. Reese felt out of place amongst the peerage in their fancy plumage. He wished Fanny were here. She'd know what to do. Where was Nick?

"Ah! Look who's coming. Viscount Wharncliffe." He smiled down at Beth. "You'll like Lord Wharncliffe. Salt of the earth. Sold his commission when his younger brother died. He's . . ." Reese stopped before mentioning the five nephews. Nick and Ardmoor strongly urged the nephews not be mentioned until she and Nick were betrothed. "... a good man."

Beth arched her brow at him. "Are you trying to marry me off?"

Reese patted her hand. *Please God. Please.* "You know I can't force you to marry, Beth." It had been discussed amongst the men, though. The more port they drank the more expansive and imaginative their plans. "But should you happen to meet someone suitable, you know Fanny and I would be happy for you." Her eyes narrowed and he leaned close to whisper. "Don't try to scare him away with talk about your culinary passion. He knows you love to cook. It intrigued him." Seeing her blink and look closer as Nick approached, he allowed himself a smug smile. Damn if Ardmoor didn't know women!

* * * *

Nick fought to keep a grin off his face as he gazed upon the vision next to Reese. Ardmoor said she was attractive, and said his sister, the Countess of Spode, approved the chit, extolling her wit and charm. Reese's sister was more than attractive, she was beautiful! A vision of beauty who was charming, appreciated good food, even so far as to cook it herself, and possessed a large dowry!

Nick smiled as the introductions were made. Miss Reese was petite, the top of her curls reaching his chin. Pity, he liked height in a woman. But she was shapely. Her hair was light brown, done up in curls with ribbons or some such woven through; made him want to see it down. Her eyes were large, and though he couldn't be sure, he thought they might be hazel. He would make a point of determining their exact color at a later time. Tomorrow, perhaps, when they drove around the park. Now, however, he needed to begin his campaign. Two weeks were lost because Ardmoor's sister insisted Miss Reese be fitted for new clothes. Not at all a waste of time, he amended as he took in her appearance.

"Do you dance, Miss Reese?"

"I do, Lord Wharncliffe. I've been known to dance a jig whilst waiting for my bread to rise."

Nick smiled and then blinked, wondering if he's heard correctly. She slowly fanned her face as she looked over the crowd. Then looked back at him. "That was a jest, my lord."

Nick looked at Reese, but the man's eyes were closed as he shook his head. Nick cleared his throat and smiled at Miss Reese. "I should have known. I'd heard you had wit." The corners of her eyes crinkled as she looked to be fighting a smile. She fanned a little harder.

"I have been the subject of conversation, my lord?" She poked her brother with her fan. "Will, did you hear? Lord Wharncliffe says I've been the object of—"

"Go dance with the man, Beth," her brother ordered.

* * * *

Beth was prepared to dislike the man her brother selected for her. Even the Countess of Spode's assurance that Viscount Wharncliffe was not a man to be lightly dismissed failed to turn her mind. He was, after all, a man who needed a wife with a large dowry. That he would overlook her passion for the kitchen—a low class and common preoccupation her brother informed her—merely pointed out Lord Wharncliffe's desperation. She assumed any woman would do.

Her first sight of him upset her preconceived notions; a tall, dark and striking man, his face finely chiseled, rugged yet attractive. He was so good-looking she blinked to make sure her sight was true. She wondered that this man was in need of a wife. Although he was handsome in his black coat and breeches, she could imagine how magnificent his physique looked in dress uniform. She would have to discover what was wrong with him; didn't think it would take long.

But when he took her hand in his, and she looked into his grey eyes, Beth felt the physical shock of which the Countess of Spode had spoken. The awareness of a man. She cautioned Beth not to agree to any match unless she felt her body unaccountably wanting to pitch itself into the arms of her betrothed. Beth had laughed, thinking it one of the countess's jests, but now she understood. Oh my, yes.

When he touched her hands, or her arm when they danced, Beth's body reacted with tingles and warmth. It was disconcerting, yet, at the same time, Beth enjoyed the waves of awareness. As if her body had been sleeping, waiting for this man to come and awaken her.

They danced twice, and he asked if he might call upon her the next day and take her for a drive in the park. Her brother answered for her, even before Lord Wharncliffe finished speaking, but Lord Wharncliffe repeated his request, this time directed to her. She said yes.

Chapter Two
The Courtship Begins

The drive went well. Nick enjoyed being seen in the company of such an attractive woman as Miss Reese. Judging from the flowers he'd seen in the drawing room when waiting for her earlier, her appearance last evening made a favorable impression on other men as well. Pity he left early, but it was never wise to leave the monsters alone for long. He'd have to have a word with Reese, make sure the man understood his sister would be his viscountess as soon as she agreed to the match. No need for other men to attend her.

When she made mention of her interest in entering the Annual Allied Victory Celebration for the Benefit of Our Maimed Soldiers Best Recipe Contest, Nick didn't know if it was another one of her humorous quips or if she were serious. If serious, he knew the dish to assure her of winning. And if she won, and won due to *his* help, surely that would count in his favor.

Now they were at Gunter's, having an ice. Nick silently congratulated himself for thinking of the place. It was pleasant to sit across from her, soothing to listen to her voice, and watch her lick her spoon. Imagined her lips wrapped around . . . His attention snapped back to her words.

* * * *

"I said, it must be difficult for a man to be confronted with the care and raising of five nephews. I understand you sold your commission to return home and assume responsibility for them. It must have been quite an adjustment." Beth sucked harder on her spoon to keep from laughing. The man's expression was a cross between horror and embarrassment, although he still managed to look handsome.

"You know about the . . .?" Viscount Wharncliffe closed his eyes.

"The five nephews, yes. The Countess of Spode apprised me of the fact. She spoke highly of you, my lord, but said I should be aware you had the care of your brother's children. Two sets of twins? How do you manage?" Beth wondered at the strange smile on his face.

"That's all she said? About the boys, that is."

"She said they were difficult for you to manage."

Lord Wharncliffe nodded. "Difficult."

Beth looked down as she swirled the ice in her dish. She wished the viscount would be more forthcoming. She understood her brother was promoting this match, and since meeting Viscount Wharncliffe her many objections to marriage were dwindling. But she did want to know more about the man who might be her husband. Other than he was the most attractive man she'd ever met, with his dark hair and grey eyes, and was a pleasant conversationalist, she had no idea what his beliefs might be, how he viewed life, or what made him different from any other wickedly handsome viscount who needed a rich wife. She almost didn't hear his next words.

"Monsters."

"Beg pardon?"

"They're monsters. Unruly hellions, the lot of them. Can't keep a housekeeper or cook. They sneak into the pantry and larder and eat whatever's been set aside. Delight in scaring the maids. Climb to the roof and throw things at people. Can't have guests." He sighed and shook his head.

Beth didn't know whether or not he was serious. "How old are they?"

Lord Wharncliffe exhaled heavily. "The oldest is nine. No, ten. The first twins are eight. The second twins are six." The lop-sided smile he gave her spread warmth in her chest. "Now you know."

Beth half-laughed. "Now I know what? They sound like normal boys with no supervision."

Lord Wharncliffe arched a dark brow at her, and her stomach flipped in response. The way his dark lashes framed his eyes when he cocked a brow was lethal. "I was in the army, Miss Reese. I know about discipline. These boys are monsters."

Beth set down her spoon, all thoughts of Lord Wharncliffe's handsomeness put aside. "My lord, army discipline is fine for grown men, but we are speaking of boys! No doubt they snuck in to the larder and pantry because they were hungry. Having fed and raised two younger brothers and one sister, I can assure you, the bodies of the young require large quantities of food!" Realizing what she'd said, Beth's face grew warm. "I beg your pardon if I offended."

He stared at her as if she had uttered something incomprehensible. She looked away and back to his face. Doubtless she *had* offended. Well, there it was then. The courtship over before it began. It was for the best though, if he took umbrage, because she'd spoken her mind. Then he smiled. "You have not offended, Miss Reese."

At the sight of his smile, her face warmed again, while her stomach flipped. She smiled as well.

"Tell me how it came about that you had the care of your younger siblings, Miss Reese."

* * * *

Nick knew she was the one. This was the woman with whom he'd willingly leg-shackle himself. The longer he listened and heard her opinions, the surer he became. She was no school room miss without an original thought to express, voicing no opinion unless upon clothing or gossip, who desired nothing more than an advantageous marriage, a house in town and a carriage. She—whose mother was the daughter of an earl, and whose father the second son of a baron—evinced no anger or resentment, other than a dismissive huff, over her mother's family disowning her mother and her mother's children.

Miss Reese admitted she favored the country over London. She enjoyed teaching children to read, and did so each Sunday in her village. Saw no shame with her delight in creating delicious meals—but said she'd twigged her brother about it being her consuming passion. "He's so easy to tease," she confessed with a smile. He liked how she made him laugh. Her lack of height he now considered an asset. The image of her in his arms or beneath him was never far from his thoughts.

Nick looked forward to having her smile be the first thing he saw in the morning. Knew he'd enjoy conversing with her at night, or sitting with her in companionable silence. Then, of course, there was the prospect of her beneath him, day, night, at all hours, once they wed.

With that image in mind, Nick handed her into his phaeton. Time for serious wooing.

"What is that grin about, my lord?" Miss Reese asked. "If we both didn't know my brother would shoot you should any insult be done to me, I might be fearful at the sight of those teeth showing."

Nick arched his brow. "I am wooing you, Miss Reese. I can't help but smile and grin like a bedlamite."

Chapter Three
Vile Sauerkraut and Other Worries

Beth and the Countess of Spode exchanged glances, the countess giving Beth a smug smile before telling the footman to admit Viscount Wharncliffe.

"How did he know I was here?" Beth asked.

"Didn't I just finish saying Lord Wharncliffe is near declaring for you?" the countess replied. "The man wants you. Therefore, he will make it his business to know where and with whom you spend your time." The countess narrowed her eyes at Beth. "Are you displeased by his attention?"

Beth laughed and shook her head. "Heavens, no! On the contrary, I am amazed such a man would take interest in *me*."

The countess smiled. "You are worthy of Wharncliffe, Beth, and he of you. The perfect match."

"Do not jinx me so! Nothing is perfect."

The countess inclined her head. "Let me say then, I believe you two will do well together. Yours will be a marriage of mutual attraction and appreciation for each other's strengths and abilities."

Beth leaned close to whisper when she heard steps drawing near. "Eight days since we were introduced, and I have seen him every day. Each day I feel more strongly the urge to . . . to grab hold of him and kiss him!" She looked to see the countess's reaction.

The countess nodded, a soft smile on her face as she rubbed her swollen belly. "Yes."

"I always remember myself in time," Beth said. "Besides, I've never kissed a man on the lips. I'm not sure . . ." Beth pulled herself upright when Lord Wharncliffe was announced.

For a moment he remained in the doorway. Taller than most men, his physique was well muscled but not heavy. Beth appreciated his wavy, dark hair, but she considered his eyes framed with thick, dark lashes one of his finer points. It was Lord Wharncliffe's smile, however, and especially when the smile was directed at her, that caused Beth to consider throwing herself into his arms. Madness!

The madness-causing smile fastened on her. "How is the recipe creating coming along?"

Beth didn't allow herself to slump. "I believe sauerkraut may be an acquired taste, my lord."

The countess looked between Beth and Lord Wharncliffe. "Sauerkraut? What is that?"

"Shredded cabbage fermented in its own juice," Beth replied. "Vile," she muttered.

The countess looked from Beth to Lord Wharncliffe. "You expect her to win a recipe contest with fermented cabbage?"

Lord Wharncliffe took a seat. "I've heard that not only will the Prussian ambassador be judging, but the queen as well. I have it on good authority they both love dishes made with sauerkraut. Surely anything Miss Reese makes with sauerkraut will win." He turned to Beth. "Have you created a sauerkraut masterpiece of culinary perfection yet?"

Beth forced a smile to her lips. "I'm working on a few ingredient changes." Tears were not far away, however. Lord Wharncliffe was a dear to go to all this bother for her, not only filing her application for her, but supporting her decision to enter. She didn't think most men would consider helping her the way he had, a large point in his favor. He was positive she would win with *sauerkraut,* while Beth was certain she would be hooted and scorned should she present the nasty, fermented cabbage to the judges. What *was* she to do?

* * * *

"Fanny? Am I disturbing you?" Beth stepped inside the darkened room. "I've brought you a little something to eat." She winced at Fanny's answering moan. "It's all bland, just the way you instructed."

"You didn't add anything this time?" Fanny's faint voice asked from where she lay on her bed.

"Not a thing. Oh, Fanny, I am sorry for doubting you and Will. Do you forgive me?"

Fanny removed the cloth from her eyes and looked at her. "You no longer believe my increasing is a lie, a ploy to get you to London and foist you off on some repellant older man?"

Beth bit her bottom lip and shook her head. "I'm sorry, Fanny. Although I know you and Will do want me out of the house—"

"We don't want you out, we want—"

"I understand," Beth said as she set the tray on the table next to the bed. "You want your own home. I *do* understand, really. I want that, too." She smiled at the thought of Lord Wharncliffe. "Do not repeat to Will what I'm about to tell you, but I'm rather taken with Viscount Wharncliffe."

"Oh, I'm so happy for you, Beth! When I heard he'd paid such particular attention to you, I told Will it wouldn't be long before the banns were read." Fanny smiled and grasped Beth's hand. "He was always such a gentleman. Pretty manners, and so considerate of others. Oh, Beth, you couldn't ask for a finer man as husband."

Beth laughed. "Well, he hasn't asked me yet. Which brings me to another point. One of two, actually. Lord Wharncliffe assisted me in entering the Annual Allied Victory Celebration for the Benefit of Our Maimed Soldiers Best Recipe Contest. Do you think that will anger Will? Not only did Lord Wharncliffe urge me to enter, he told me *what* to enter. Although I shan't tell you what it is as I am positive it would cause you to cast up your accounts. Lord Wharncliffe says he's delighted by my joy in creating, be it food or poetry or art. I think that's rather sweet. But sometimes I'm not sure I should believe him. Suppose he's saying that to lull me into trusting him so I'll agree to marry him and doesn't believe that at all? Suppose we marry and then he—"

"There was another point, you said?"

Beth held her hand to her forehead. Lord, but she sounded like a ninny! "Yes. I've never met Lord Wharncliffe's nephews. Don't you think that odd? We aren't betrothed, true, but I do think he might have introduced us. Suppose they don't like me?" Beth inhaled sharply. "Suppose he knows they won't like me!" Beth looked at Fanny when she heard her groan. "What can I get you, Fanny?"

"Beth, his nephews will adore you. Bake them jam tarts or lemon biscuits or some such treats. All boys can be bribed with food."

"Tarts, yes. I'm good with tarts."

"Beth, I've known Lord Wharncliffe for far longer than you. Believe whatever Lord Wharncliffe tells you."

Beth nodded. "Yes, Fanny."

Chapter Four
Nick Comes to a Decision

"You what?" Nick asked. Judging from Miss Reese's startled expression, he deduced his tone may have been a tad strident. Nick cleared his throat and smiled. "That is to say, what prompted you to go to such lengths?" He looked at the two large, overflowing baskets sitting on a table in the drawing room. She must have been baking since dawn. No, the entire kitchen must have been baking since dawn. "You shouldn't have gone to such trouble for my nephews. They've been quite happy with twice daily raids—er, visits to the sweet shop and bakery." His gaze shifted back to the sight of Miss Reese clasping her hands, a small frown creasing her forehead. Surely not a good sign. He was making a muddle of this, but her announcing she'd made treats for his nephews caught him off guard. If he didn't handle this carefully, she might want to *meet* them. He intended they be safely betrothed before that happened. "I'm sure the boys will be delighted with the efforts of your thoughtfulness." He could well imagine the little monsters circling him, little hands and arms clawing their way to the food, wolfing down the contents before the baskets were set down.

She smiled. "Do you ever take them to the park, my lord?"

Nick knew what was coming. Other than sweeping her into his arms and kissing her senseless, he didn't know how to avoid this.

"I go daily with my maid. If you and your nephews are in the habit of enjoying the park, it occurred to me we might . . ."

Sweeping her into his arms and kissing her senseless would come soon, but first things first. Time to get Major Reese's formal consent. "Is your brother at home, Miss Reese?" Damn, she was frowning again. He inhaled sharply. Did he have it wrong? Could it be she wanted to meet his nephews because she was inclined to accept him as a suitor?

"My brother? I believe Will is out, but—"

"Miss Reese," Nick said as he stepped before her and took her warm hands in his. "Your brother gave me permission to court you. We've seen each other daily for three weeks, or near enough it doesn't matter. I've tried wooing you to the best of my ability, although I admit I often don't know exactly . . . what I'm supposed to do. I thought after the Annual Victory . . . Annual Allied Victory . . . the contest—are your hands shaking, Miss Reese? As I was saying, I thought to wait until you had won the competition to ask you, but I find I cannot wait another day. Nor another hour."

Nick's gaze shifted about the room until he spied the closest seat, whereupon he escorted Miss Reese to the chair and indicated she should sit. He got down on bended knee before her.

"Miss Reese, will you do me the very great honor of accepting my proposal of marriage? I can think of no other woman I want at my side as helpmate. I offer you an old distinguished title; you would be my viscountess, Viscountess Wharncliffe. Also an old drafty home in Yorkshire, but it will be made warm with you there as my wife. There are other properties, not at all drafty, but my brother insisted his children be raised at Gorse Grange." Nick fell silent, his mind gone blank, unable to remember what else he had to offer her. "Ah! You have my admiration for your . . ." He fell silent when he looked into her eyes. Hazel eyes that could change from blue to green to grey. Those eyes were now large and bright and shining. "Are you crying? Does that mean you don't—"

"Silly man."

* * * *

Beth's emotions had run the gamut. Fear she appeared too forward by baking treats for his nephews. Anger when she thought he dismissed her. Joy when she realized he was asking her to marry him. Happiness when she understood she wanted to marry this man. He was babbling again.

"You haven't answered me," he said.

She smiled. It was impossible not to. "Yes, my lord, I accept your proposal of marriage."

"Nick," he said as he raised her hands to his mouth. "My name is Nick. Will you say my name?"

"Nick," she said. "My name is—"

"Elizabeth. I shall call you Lizzy."

Beth laughed. "If you do I shall ignore you. Or call you Nicholas." She stuck out her tongue. "So there! When will I meet—"His face loomed close.

"Now that you have accepted me, I'm entitled to a kiss."

She was glad she was sitting, as her insides turned to warm mush. "You want to kiss me?" Her bones melted when he grinned at her.

"Definitely." His hands cupped her face. "A claiming kiss, if you will."

Beth didn't have long to wonder what a claiming kiss might be. His lips settled on hers, and she was surprised how soft they were. They moved on hers, back and forth until she followed along. Something warm and soft pressed against her closed lips, tickling them. She opened her mouth and felt his tongue enter. She had no idea such a disgusting concept could feel so good. Was *she* allowed to use her tongue? Beth touched the tip of her tongue to his and he groaned and pulled her closer, deepening his kiss. Obviously she did the right thing. She knew kissing would be a pleasurable part of marriage. "Oh my," she whispered when he pulled away. The way he stared so intently into her eyes, it appeared as though an inner debate was raging.

"You'll have to meet them," Nick finally said. "My honor insists you meet them before we go further with our betrothal."

* * * *

Five pair of eyes, eyes in varying shades of grey and blue looked back at him. Crumbs stuck to their mouths, chin, nose and hair. Nick no longer wondered how they managed to get food in their ears. "Do you understand me? You will be polite to her."

"Suppose she doesn't like us?"

"Suppose we don't like her?"

"Will we have food like this all the time if she marries you?"

"What do we call her?"

"Will she send us off to school? Jones said naughty boys are starved at school."

Nick knew it important his nephews believe he wouldn't abandon them. That they understood their future was secure and they would remain with him, that he wouldn't be unduly influenced by his coming marriage. He answered each question put to him until he realized he was answering what they would name their new puppies.

"We have puppies at the grange and you've already named them. Now, do I have your word you will be nice to Miss Reese? If you scare her off, she won't want to marry me. Then you won't get any more treats like the ones you've just devoured."

* * * *

"I'm sorry I cannot join you, Beth," Fanny said.

Beth wiped her sister-in-law's mouth and handed the bowl to the maid. "I think it best you remain abed, Fanny. The countess said she would be here before they all arrive."

"I've not been much of a chaperone for you, have I?"

"I have not minded." Beth grinned when she thought of Nick's claiming kiss. And the ones after that. "Besides, I've been busy with my celebration recipe. I believe I finally found a way to make the dish edible."

"What did you do?"

Beth wagged a finger. "I never give away my secrets. And if I told you what I was making, we'd need the bowl again." She leaned over and gave Fanny a kiss on the cheek. "Wish me luck with the boys. Lord Wharncliffe seems to think I might bow out of my agreement once I meet his nephews."

* * * *

Nick knew the time for more cautionary words had passed. He and his five nephews were in the drawing room. Beth and the Countess of Spode were in attendance. Introductions had been made, and his nephews sat and fidgeted. So far, so good.

"When I heard you liked what I baked for you," Beth said as she smiled at the boys, "I decided to make more for you today."

Nick sat straighter, visions of food flying, his nephews fighting and scrambling to get every last crumb. "I don't . . ."

Beth leaned toward the boys. "Since we're in my brother's drawing room, and not the nursery, you must remember to use your best manners. Were you taught about good manners?"

Jason, the eldest, spoke. "Our mother said we had the best manners of any boys she ever knew."

Nick lifted his brows, but remained silent.

Beth smiled and nodded. "I thought so. Are you hungry?"

Nick snorted. *When weren't they hungry?*

* * * *

"I think it went very well," Beth said. "They are adorable boys!"

Nick shrugged and smiled. "You have no idea how happy it makes me to hear you say that," he said, while inside he was whooping with joy. "Now that you've met them, and you agree to marry me, it's time to set a date." He looked to see if they were alone before pulling her close and setting his lips to hers. Her mouth was warm and tasted of lemon tart. He heard himself groan when his lips came off hers. "You don't want a large wedding, do you? We don't want to wait for months, do we?" To his surprise, Beth pulled his head down and kissed him before she spoke.

"No. I just want to win the Annual Allied Victory Celebration contest, but that's only one week away."

Nick pulled back to look at her. "Winning means that much to you?"

"Winning this competition, yes, for I've never had as much trouble with a recipe as I had with sauerkraut. More than that, when and if I win, I shall win as Miss Elizabeth Reese. That's who I am. That's who concocted my recipe. Once we wed, I shall be Viscountess Wharncliffe."

Little ripples of alarm went down his spine. "If you don't win, does that mean—" Her finger rested across his lips.

"I shall win. I have created something delicious. Not an easy task when one is working with fermented cabbage."

She certainly sounded confident. Nick sucked her finger into his mouth before kissing its tip. "Then be prepared to set the date after your victory next week."

Chapter Five
Sweet Victory

Nick found her conversing with the countess and Ardmoor. "Beth, may I have a word with you?" He escorted her a few feet away, his heart heavy with regret. "I'm so sorry, Beth. I just learned the queen isn't judging, nor the Prussian ambassador." His chest tightened when he saw her eyes grow large. "Worse, the Regent is a judge. He hates anything with sauerkraut. I'm so sorry."

She put a hand to her chest and smiled. "You frightened me for a moment."

"Didn't you hear me? The Regent hates anything with sauerkraut!"

"Not to worry," Beth said. "He is reputed to be an epicure. He will love my creation."

Nick admired a healthy dose of optimism, but feared his Beth was deluding herself. He wished he'd never encouraged her to enter.

"The bloody show's about to begin," Ardmoor whispered in his ear. "Heard about the change in judges. Bloody good thing she already agreed to wed you."

Nick nodded. He shouldn't have helped her. Who knew how long this disappointment might affect her? Might she be so disappointed when she lost, she'd postpone their nuptials?

* * * *

Beth smiled and looked down at the floor. She knew she was blushing, the tell-tale warmth rising up past her ears. The clapping was loud, she thought particularly loud coming from Nick and Ardmoor. No, it was Ardmoor stomping his wooden leg on the floor generating the most noise. Nick's face was flushed and his grin went from ear to ear. It was sweet of him to be so happy for her.

She'd won. All the judges had looked at her dish and frowned, two even sniggered. Had the contest rules not explicitly stated the judges must try a mouthful, she doubted any would have sampled her dish. Not that she blamed them. Sauerkraut was vile. But her sauerkraut—Sweet Sauerkraut as she named her recipe—was delicious. All had agreed. She won first prize in Most Unusual Dish, first prize in Allied Recipe and first prize in the Surprisingly Good Dish.

The ribbons she would cherish. Today's triumph she would remember for the rest of her life.

Even the Regent spoke to her after, asking what it was she did to make the sauerkraut edible.

"After it ferments, I rinse it well, Your Grace. Then I melt butter in a pan and cook the drained cabbage until it isn't soggy."

"Spices?" he asked.

"Pepper and a pinch of salt."

He shook his head. "Amazing."

"Oh no, Your Grace," Beth said. "It is the butter. Adding butter to anything improves the taste."

* * * *

"You won, Beth," Nick said. "You did it!" His chest was near to bursting, he was so proud of her.

"You sound surprised."

"I am. I never understood how people could eat the stuff. But you! *You* created a winning recipe with fermented cabbage leaves. Amazing!" He smiled when she blushed. They still had the ribbon ceremony to attend, and the formal handing over the proceeds to the Maimed Soldiers foundation before they could leave. He wanted to be alone with her, show her in more intimate detail how proud he was of her. They were betrothed, after all.

"The Regent said I must enter next year."

Nick's gaze traveled the room until he saw the prince in a far corner. The regent nodded and smiled in his direction. Nick felt a growl rise in his throat, and he moved to block Beth from his sight. It was on the tip of his tongue to inform her it would be over his dead body before he again allowed her near the Regent's lascivious gaze.

"I told him I would doubtless be in Yorkshire this time next year."

Nick's attention snapped back to her. He smiled. "You did?" His smile broadened when she blushed and looked down. "Did you tell him you'd be working on the bread in your oven?"

Beth looked up, her brow creased. "Bread in my oven?"

Nick waggled his brows. "You know. Warming the bread in your oven." When she cocked her head at him, he leaned and whispered in her ear.

"Oh!" she said when she stepped back, her faced suffused with a rosy blush. "My lord! Nick!"She glanced around. Before he knew what she was about, she stepped near, pulled down his head as if to whisper a reply. The touch of her warm tongue in his ear—brief as it was—nearly caused him to shout. The girl learned quickly.

"The banns," Nick said as he looked deep into her eyes, "must be read soon."

Her gaze traveled his face, from his eyes to his lips, lingering on his lips before returning to his eyes. "My brother is having them read this Sunday at our church back home."

"So we'll wed in three weeks?"

She licked her lips before she spoke. *Did she realize what that did to him?* "Yes."

"Good. You are due another claiming kiss." He smiled when her eyes widened. "Something a little different this time. Wicked," he whispered. Her pupils dilated. "You shall like it."

"I am sure I will," she whispered. They turned when her name was called.

She gave him a small smile before turning to walk to the podium.

"I'm proud of you, Beth," he called after her.

She turned, a look of surprise on her face. A blush rose on her cheeks. Then she smiled, a smile that suffused her face with joy. The happiness showing on her face flooded his chest with warmth. Nick knew he'd gladly spend the rest of his life keeping her smiling as she was this day, just as he knew she would continue making him proud of her.

"Bloody well done, Nick," Ardmoor said as he slapped him on the back. "Sweet sauerkraut, indeed. Bloody well done, the both of you!"

~~~

Sweet Sauerkraut

Ingredients needed:

1 can or jar of sauerkraut, near 20 ounces
1 ½ stick of BUTTER
Pinch of salt
Pepper to taste

Drain and rinse sauerkraut in sieve with cold water. Drain excess water.

Melt butter in skillet and add drained sauerkraut, stirring occasionally until some of the sauerkraut looks a little fried. Add pinch of salt if desired, and pepper to taste.

Can be made ahead and reheated in oven until hot.

Joy's Christmas Wishes

Chapter One
Joy's Two Wishes

"Lady Emily, do you like my father?" Joy hopped from one foot to the other as they walked outside. "You met him in London, did you not? He's coming here for Christmas. He promised."

Emily had no trouble calling to mind the handsome image of Captain Geoffrey DeBohun—immediately replaced by the snarling face of a father who thought his children had been taken from him. Emily shuddered at the recollection of the unpleasant encounter, brief as it had been. Whatever might be said of Captain DeBohun, the paternal instinct to protect and defend his children was fully developed. She smiled at the eleven-year-old girl beside her.

"Yes, I met him in London. He thought his brother, Wickerdun, had absconded with you and your brothers. He was most upset."

Joy giggled. "Now he knows we still live with my aunt, just in a different house since she and your brother married." Joy stopped and looked up at her. "I'm going to make Christmas wishes. My mother told us there are special times when wishes would be granted."

"Oh?" Emily cringed inside. From the moment she met Joy, well over a year ago, the child had fixated on the idea she should marry her father. Although pleased Joy considered her a potential stepmother, Emily believed any woman presented to Joy would have been a candidate. She hoped Joy wouldn't wish for what couldn't be. "Be careful what you wish for, dear. You must not waste your wishes."

Joy shook her head. "I have thought about my wishes. I even asked Simon, Hunter and Henry, and they all agree with me."

Oh dear. She'd consulted with her brothers.

"I wish for my father to stay home, and never go out on a ship again unless he takes us with him. Oh, look!" Joy cried as she pointed to the sky. The stars were just beginning to come out. "Look, the stars are twinkling." Joy hopped up and down. "That means I get my wish!"

"What a lovely—"

"That was just my first wish." Joy looked into her eyes. "My second wish is for you to be my new mother. If you married my father, you would make him laugh and then he wouldn't want to sail away on a ship. He would make you happy, I know, because Aunt Maddy says he made my mother very happy."

Emily smiled. "That's because they loved one another, dearest. Love does not—"

"Look! The stars are twinkling again! You're going to be my new mother!"

Emily nearly toppled over from the force of Joy's enthusiastic hug.

* * * *

"There, see, the last of your bloody brood is accounted for," Ardmoor said to his brother-in-law as they rounded the terrace. "Told you Joy would be with Lady Emily. Maddy says they never need look beyond Emily to find Joy." Ardmoor paused to allow Geoffrey his usual admonishment about his language, then looked to see why Geoffrey remained silent. "Like a bloody leech," Ardmoor added, tapping his peg leg for emphasis, wondering if he'd get a response. But no, Geoffrey's gaze remained on his daughter and Lady Emily. Ardmoor was certain the pole-axed look on Geoffrey's face was due to Lady Emily's laughter and large smile as she hugged Joy. Not to be wondered at, the woman was attractive. *Interesting.*

The voices of Spode, his sister Maddy's husband, and Wickerdun, Geoffrey's older brother, broke the silence, and looked to pull Geoffrey from his reverie. Ardmoor looked back at the new arrivals, recalling that Spode promoted a match between Wickerdun and his sister, Lady Emily. *Oh, very interesting. Brother against brother for the fair hand of Lady Emily?*

* * * *

"Look who is here, Joy. Zounds, Em, but Joy is your veritable shadow!"

Emily looked up at the sound of her brother's voice, but her sight focused on Captain DeBohun. His gaze was fast upon her. Emily couldn't tell what he meant by such an intent stare. Was he angry because she and Joy were sharing each other's company? She was grateful for Joy's squeal of delight upon seeing her father, for it broke the contact between her and Captain DeBohun.

"Papa!" Joy cried as she hugged her father. "I told Lady Emily you were coming! You promised, so I knew you'd be here for Christmas." She drew back and looked at his face. "How long will you stay?"

"How long would you like, princess?" he asked as he knelt before his daughter.

Emily watched and listened, amazed that the surly, rude man of her recollection could transform himself into the smiling, soft-spoken father before her.

"Forever, Papa. We all want you to stay home. Even Simon and Hunter agree, and you know they always wanted to go sailing with you. Will you? Will you stop sailing your ship and stay home? Please?"

Emily inhaled sharply when Captain DeBohun smiled The man was heartbreakingly handsome when he smiled. She almost missed his next words.

"Yes, princess, I'm home to stay."

When the child turned and looked at her, Emily was positive her eyes must be as wide as Joy's. "You see, Lady Emily! I told you my wishes would come true!"

The captain looked from his daughter to her. Emily lifted her chin at his raised brows. He looked back at his daughter.

"Why aren't you in the schoolroom, Joy?"

"Papa!" Joy giggled. "It's Christmas! Miss Hanson went home to her family."

"The girl has attached herself to Lady Emily," Ardmoor drawled.

When Joy's father looked at her, Emily fought the urge to press her hand to her breast. Drat! She pulled her hand away from her chest.

"Has my daughter been incommodious, Lady Emily?"

"Not at all. Joy is a delightful girl. She's—"

"She's my daughter, Lady Emily," he said as he rose.

Emily's chin rose higher. "I'm perfectly aware—"

"Papa, Lady Emily said she would be pleased if I kept her company," Joy said as she pulled her father's hand. "I like her and she likes me, and I wish—"

"Joy!" Emily exclaimed. "You must take your father to the barn. Remember what you and your brothers wanted him to see?"

"Perhaps tomorrow," Spode said. "Time we head inside. I declare, it's cold enough the lake will surely freeze this night! Emily, allow Wickerdun to escort—"

"Oh please!" Joy interrupted as she danced from one foot to the next and turned her big, blue eyes to her relatively new uncle. "I want my father to walk with me and Lady Emily. Please?"

"Zounds!" Spode turned and smiled at everyone. "Can't resist so sweet a request now, can I? Of course your father and Emily will walk with you."

Emily placed her hand on the arm presented to her, while her other hand was gripped by a determined little girl.

Chapter Two
First Impressions Prove False

The men didn't remain long in the dining room with their after dinner port, for which Geoffrey was grateful. It appeared the Earl of Spode was unabashedly in love with his wife, and deliriously proud she'd presented him with an heir four months ago. He declared he preferred his countess' company to that of cigar-smoking, liquor-swilling men. Geoffrey understood that. He was glad Maddy, his former sister-in-law, had wed a man who cared more for her than convention's dictates.

Geoffrey's gaze fastened on Lady Emily as soon as he and the other men entered the drawing room. She was seated next to Maddy, now the Countess of Spode. The two women spoke, but Geoffrey saw Lady Emily dart glances at him as he approached. He wondered if she might actually take flight if he addressed her. Ladies of her ilk seldom did more than gaze appreciatively at men of his kind—attractive yes, but a second son, captain of his own ship, a merchant, widowed, with four children. Since his brother had informed him an announcement of marriage might come from this visit, Geoffrey knew Lady Emily was forbidden to him. It mattered not. She'd avoided his gaze and conversation with him at dinner, which made Geoffrey perversely want to press her. Make her look him in the eye. Respond to him. She had no right to look so attractive. To cause his blood to heat when she looked him in the eye. Just like Laurel used to do.

"Well, Geoffrey," Maddy began, "I'm pleased by your decision to give up your sailing days and remain home with your children, where you belong. The boys have need of a father who will be present for them as they mature, not wandering about the world sailing the seven seas."

Geoffrey arched a brow. "I'd nearly forgotten how you're so effortlessly able to express your opinion, Maddy. I am duly chastised."

Maddy chuckled. "As if you ever listened to me."

"Oh, I listened," he replied, his eyes shifting to Lady Emily. She looked away. He looked back to his sister-in-law. "I just didn't always agree."

"Well, the children are ecstatic, especially Joy. Emily told me Joy made a Christmas wish for you to remain at home, and not long after, her wish came true!"

Geoffrey caught Emily's eyes. His pulse thrummed loud in his ears as he gazed into her eyes. What the devil was their color? He'd have sworn they were blue when he found her outside with Joy. Now they looked dark. "Is that so, Lady Emily?" He wasn't aware eyes could get so large.

"Yes," Emily replied, but had trouble holding his gaze. "She spoke her wish aloud and not long after, she said the stars twinkled at her. She was quite happy. I was afraid—"

"Afraid she'd be disappointed?"

The way she blushed to the roots of her hair was charming. Brown hair. He'd never been fond of brown hair on a woman, but Lady Emily's hair looked soft. Puffy, not pulled back tight the way so many women wore their hair. Inviting to the touch. He judged it was long, possibly down to her hips, and tried to picture what she'd look like with it loose and flowing. Her voice jerked him back to the present. Had he been gawking?

"Well, yes. Children do get their hopes up, and are often disappointed. I didn't want Joy to be disappointed. Yet . . ."

Geoffrey's gaze focused on her lips, seeing her bite on the lower lip and suck it in. His pulse thrummed harder. "Yet?"

"We can't always have what we wish for, can we?"

Geoffrey shook his head. He had no idea what she was referring to, and was grateful for his brother and Spode's approach. The urge to pull Lady Emily into his arms was almost overpowering. The same urge he'd had when he met Laurel.

* * * *

Emily despised herself for not ignoring Geoffrey's presence. Loathed how she watched his movements as he ranged around the room. Scorned herself for trying to hear his conversation. What was wrong with her?

She'd had two Seasons in London, both successful. Her first when she was eighteen. Four years later, when she put away her mourning clothes, she had her second Season. Countless men had vied for her attention, attempted to woo her; she'd felt nothing. At age twenty-three, she was no green girl dazzled by the first handsome man to look at her twice. Why then was her attention so focused on him? No, more than that.

An overpowering urge to gaze deep and long into his grey eyes. Touch his face. Hear him speak about his life, from childhood to manhood. To know everything about him. She wanted to be captured in his arms. Wanted him to kiss her. What was wrong with her? It was his brother, the Earl of Wickerdun, she was supposed to be considering as a husband.

Wickerdun was a large man, like her brother. Taller, broader than most men. Geoffrey was only an inch or so shorter in stature, but still over six feet. And his chest was broad. She thought that might be due to setting sails or steering the wheel, or whatever it was that sea captains did. Fighting pirates? Had he ever fought pirates? Or the French or Americans? She'd love to hear those tales! Drat! Her attention should be focused on Wickerdun, not his brother.

It was so difficult. She'd known Wickerdun forever. Remembered him from when she'd been a young girl. She liked him, she really did. Oh, bother! How could she be expected to consider wedding Wickerdun when his brother was flaunting his broad chest, handsome looks and devastating smile in front of her?

"Lady Emily?"

Emily turned her head to see Wickerdun staring at her, his head tilted to the side. "Yes?"

"I asked if you would like me to turn the pages whilst you delight us by taking a turn at the pianoforte."

Had he spoken and she'd not heard? Judging from the faces of her brother and Maddy, she hadn't. How embarrassing! "Of course," she replied as she rose.

* * * *

Geoffrey halted upon hearing the beginning notes. He'd planned a hasty retreat before subjecting himself to an abomination of what could be termed music. But this was no idle ivory banger. Lady Emily touched the pianoforte keys not only with talent in her hands, but passion in her heart. Just as Laurel used to.

He sat silently after she'd finished, wondering if the passion he'd heard in her music was present in other parts of her life. With a shake of his head, he rose. Likely she was typical of her class and upbringing. And destined for his brother.

Emily watched Geoffrey exit the drawing room. He'd stayed while she played, but said nothing when she finished. Hadn't even applauded. Said nothing to anyone before he walked out. Why did that annoy her? He was nothing to her.

* * * *

Ardmoor edged close to his sister. "Tell your husband it won't do, Maddy. Wickerdun hasn't a bloody chance in hell. It will be Lady Emily and Geoffrey, mark my words. They couldn't keep their eyes off one another tonight."

"I know, I saw. Do you suppose Robert . . .?"

"You know Spode bloody well saw. He doesn't miss a thing."

Maddy sighed. "I don't want Emily to feel pushed into marriage with Wickerdun. Still, we may be reading more into this than we should. So they looked at one another, felt an attraction." She shrugged.

Ardmoor leaned close to his sister. "Have you known Geoffrey to look at another woman since Laurel died? No, because he hasn't. It's Lady Emily's blood." When he saw her raised brows, he continued. "You said Spode told you we share the same blood. Well, Geoffrey appears to be drawn to women who have the wild blood. Ergo, he will be overpowered by his attraction to Lady Emily's wild blood and pull a dash to the Scottish border just as he did with Laurel."

"Oh dear."

"Oh bloody dear is right! I needn't see your frown to know what your husband would think of his sister being tossed into the scandal that would ensue." Ardmoor shook his head. "Not the way to start a marriage. Not at his age."

"The day Joy met Emily, she told me that Lady Emily was going to be her new mother. Do you know the little dear made it one of her Christmas wishes?"

"Thought having her father home was her wish."

"Her first wish. Her second was having Emily as her new mother." Maddy looked at Ardmoor. "I think Laurel would approve of Emily."

"I think so, too." He grunted. "We just have to see they do this thing up the proper way. No dashing to Scotland this time."

"We can't interfere, Ardmoor! We must let them decide for themselves if they'll suit."

* * * *

"I like Wickerdun," Maddy said.

Emily sipped her morning chocolate before she spoke. *Was Maddy under orders to find out if she'd made up her mind about Wickerdun?* "Yes, he's an agreeable sort. Always has been."

"Ah, you've known him for most of your life. Robert mentioned Wickerdun always came here with him on school holiday instead of going to his own home."

"Yes. I believe Wickerdun found our home and family preferable to his own."

Maddy smiled and nodded. "Did I tell you about the first time Robert introduced me to Wickerdun? My first impression was of a fool. A pleasant fool, but a fool none-the-less."

"I believe you did tell me that story."

"He's not a fool, Emily," Maddy said as she leaned close. "He pretended to be a buffoon to put me at ease. A fine quality in a man."

"Yes." Emily finished her chocolate and rose from the table. "You may tell my brother I'm well aware of Wickerdun's fine qualities, but I haven't made up my mind."

* * * *

After learning Lord Geoffrey had gone riding, Emily judged it safe to visit the nursery, specifically Joy, without running into the girl's father. But that had to wait because Ardmoor insisted on speaking to her.

"They fell in love and before anyone knew what was what, the bl—young fools dashed to Gretna Green!" Ardmoor stomped his peg for emphasis.

Emily had heard this tale. "They were young and impetuous and in love. Your sister, Laurel, was what—all of eighteen? Lord Geoffrey not much older, surely." Emily shrugged. "It's in the past, and no good for the children to dredge it up."

"Ah, there you have it! No dashing off to Gretna Green again. Must think of the children. And your brother. Spode would bl—well, he'd surely have the man's ba—be upset if you were the subject of scandal."

What was Ardmoor implying? "I have no intention of dashing off to Gretna Green, I assure you."

"Good. All that rot about Geoffrey being a womanizer, thief, and murderer is just that—balderdash put out by his father so he could get his hands on Geoffrey's children after Laurel died. Geoffrey's a good man."

Emily arched her brow. "As good as his brother?"

Ardmoor smiled. "That's for you to decide, my dear."

Chapter Three
Lady Emily is Astounded

Due to the shrieking of the princess and the pirates, and the fact that he was the princess' personal riding dragon, Geoffrey wasn't aware of Lady Emily's presence until he realized his roar wasn't met with squeals of glee, but nervous giggles. He lifted his head and steadied the princess on his back as he sat back on his heels.

The woman's expression was priceless. Eyes opened wide in shock, her mouth agape, with her face turning redder by the moment. Likely she'd never seen the sight of a father playing with his children in the nursery.

"Lady Emily," Geoffrey said as he set Joy on her feet and rose.

"I'm sorry, I didn't think you'd—I'm sorry to intrude," she said as she stepped back.

"Just the person I wanted to see." He turned to his children. "We'll finish this later. Time to get ready for ice skating." He turned to Emily. "Would you care to join us?"

"Join you?" She looked like he was asking her to join him in plunging from the rooftop to the courtyard below.

"For ice skating. You do ice skate?"

"She's a wonderful ice skater, Papa," Joy said.

"She taught me how to spin fast!" Henry said.

"Bang up skater," Simon said.

"Top of the trees," Hunter added.

"Where do you hear such language?" Geoffrey asked. "Never mind." *Ardmoor. At least he remembers not to curse around them.* "So you'll join us, Lady Emily?" Her eyes darted from him to each of the children. "We really must talk."

"Talk?" She looked at Joy and then at him. "Er, I—"

"We'll meet you out front. Do hurry, the children are keen to skate whilst the ice is still thick enough to hold us all."

* * * *

Her eyes were like mirrors, their color hazel, reflecting whatever color dominated her sight—shades of grey, blue, green and brown. Friendly eyes. He'd swear they laughed and spoke to him, yet he needed no sound to hear. Geoffrey wanted to spend the rest of his life gazing into this woman's eyes.

Once at the pond, with the children amusing themselves, Geoffrey skated alongside Emily, careful to keep close. "Lady Emily, I apologize for my behavior when first we met. It was unconscionable. I'll not offer excuses. I know I was too quick in jumping to conclusions. I'm deeply sorry for my thoughtless words, which I know now to be false. Please accept my humblest apology."

Emily turned to him and smiled. "Oh, apology accepted. I understood later why you were so enraged. Actually . . ." She paused and Geoffrey waited for her to continue, his heart still speeding from the sight of her sudden smile. "Although you were unaccountably rude, boorish and uncivilized, I admired the fact your concern for your children caused you to act like a madman."

"You admired that?" He wished she'd turn and smile at him again.

"I did." She gave him a quick glance. "Was that what you wanted to talk to me about?"

He smiled and shook his head. "Joy told me about her wish for you and me to marry." He caught her when she lost her balance, and steadied her. "She's convinced it will be so, because she said the stars twinkled at her." He peeked at

Emily's face, hidden under a bonnet and scarf. "You needn't be embarrassed. It's not as if you put the idea into her head."

Emily looked at him in horror. "Oh, no, of course not!" she exclaimed, and promptly lost her balance. He caught her before she fell. "Thank you. The first day we met, Joy told me she wanted me to marry you so you would stay home."

"But I am staying home." He smiled when she blushed. "Her first wish, remember? Even so, she still wishes us to wed. My sons think it a splendid idea." He smiled at the quick look she darted his way. "What about you? Shall we?" This time when he caught her as she lost her balance, he pulled her down on top of him.

* * * *

"Bloody ice!"

"Careful, Ardmoor. Maddy'll have my head if you come to harm! Had to promise I'd keep an eye on you."

"Treats me like I'm a bloody china doll! I won't break if I fall! Half my leg is gone already, and the peg can be replaced."

"Surely your sister worries about the part of you that can't be replaced," Wickerdun suggested.

"Just what we need, a bloody peacemaker." Ardmoor whipped his head around at the sound of Spode's low whistle. Looked in the direction Spode and Wickerdun stared. "Bloody hell!" The two men beside him remained silent while they watched Geoffrey assist Emily to her feet. The three men continued forward.

* * * *

Geoffrey was positive she was as aroused as he. Well, perhaps not as aroused, but she was interested. There'd been no screaming for him to unhand her. No strident demands he release her. She'd stared at him with a look of wonder. His cheek still tingled where she'd touched and stroked. True, she'd been wearing mittens, but his cheek still tingled, which led him to wonder what it would feel like if her bare fingers touched and stroked. His mind conjured up a picture of her touching his bare body. Which in turn inflamed that part of him that had been idle for so long. That's when her eyes widened even more.

"I want to kiss you." It was a foolish thing to say. He realized that as soon as the words passed his lips. She struggled to rise, but collapsed and gazed into his eyes.

"Why?"

Geoffrey blinked. *Why?* "Why? Because . . . I've had the urge to pull you into my arms and kiss you from the first moment I saw you."

She drew back and arched a brow at him. "The first moment you saw me you accused me of conspiring to take your children from you. The words you used, however, were more colorful."

Geoffrey smiled and watched her eyes darken; his smile deepened. "True. But I was attracted to you, which might have angered me."

"Why should . . ."

Geoffrey looked up at the four pairs of eyes peering down at them. "We were discussing Joy's wish."

"Ooh, ooh! Has Lady Emily—"

Geoffrey broke in. "A lady's decision is never rushed, princess." He helped Emily rise, but growled softly upon spying the approach of his brother, Spode and Ardmoor.

* * * *

Emily declined all offers to escort her back to the house. Knew her face didn't stop burning until she was in sight of her home. *Everyone* had seen her lying on top of Lord Geoffrey! What was she about? Why hadn't she immediately removed herself from his person? Emily covered her cheeks with her mittened hands. *She'd felt his desire for her!* She shook her head. It had been the most thrilling experience of her life. *Ooh, but she was wanton!*

* * * *

The men gathered in Spode's library, Spode seated behind his desk, with Ardmoor and Wickerdun seated next to him. Geoffrey had the unsettling feeling of being back at school, waiting to be paddled for another *unfortunate incident.*

"Will you explain to me," Spode began, "what we saw on the lake?"

Geoffrey took a deep breath while casting about for a suitable reply that wouldn't offend. Impossible. "I asked Lady Emily to marry me. She lost her balance, and before she could fall onto the ice, I allowed her to fall on top of me." Geoffrey could swear he heard his brother's teeth grinding, but he kept his eyes on Spode. Spode's brows rose to nearly meet his hairline. "You asked my sister—"

"I bloody well saw this coming," Ardmoor declared. "Maddy and I discussed this only last evening." He nodded as three pairs of eyes swung to him. "Was obvious they couldn't keep their eyes off one another."

His brother looked at him. "Your offer for Lady Emily's hand in marriage comes rather suddenly. Why? Is it because you knew I wanted her as wife?"

"No," Geoffrey said. "No, it's nothing like that. She . . ." He shook his head, wondering if he could explain what he didn't fully understand. "I never intended to wed again. Then I met Lady Emily. I was drawn to her, but assumed her typical of her class. Too, I knew her destined for you, so I fought against the attraction. The more I saw of her, listened to her conversation, the more I realized she's different. This morning the children told me how Lady Emily has helped them since Spode and Maddy wed. How kind she is, how she tried to do the things Maddy used to do, but could no longer because of the baby. That's when I knew Lady Emily was very special. Then Joy told me about her Christmas wish for Lady Emily and me to wed, so I knew then I had to woo her and wed her."

"A Christmas wish?" Wickerdun exclaimed. "You would wed her because of a child's Christmas wish?"

"Umm," Spode said, his face creased with frowns.

"Don't make light of it, Wickerdun," Ardmoor said. "Not only is your brother drawn to Lady Emily because of her wild blood, but Joy's wish was uttered with the sincerity and purity of heart only a child can claim. Then, too, Joy has the wild blood, so that makes her wish more potent."

"And she said the star twinkled at her," Geoffrey added.

"Ah," Spode said, still frowning.

"Are you all mad?" Wickerdun asked as he looked at each man in turn.

"Not at all," Geoffrey said.

"No running to Gretna bloody Green this time," Ardmoor said.

"*What?*" Spode asked.

"Lord," Wickerdun said with a sigh, "I'd almost forgotten."

Geoffrey looked at Spode. "I wouldn't. I want a church wedding with my children present."

"I'd forgotten you'd married in Gretna Green." Spode looked from Geoffrey to Ardmoor.

"I was in the army at the time, but from what I was told, Geoffrey and my sister Laurel took one bloody look at each other and fell in love. Her first ball, and she and Geoffrey were caught on the bleeding balcony, so—"

Geoffrey cut in, "We decided not to wait, so we ran to Gretna Green. Never regretted it, the marriage that is, just the scandal it caused."

Geoffrey waited, knowing his future hung in the balance. Would the Earl of Spode allow his sister to wed him, or would he go through with plans for his sister to wed Wickerdun? Surely the man would choose Wickerdun.

And what of his brother? Geoffrey turned to look at Wickerdun. They were slowly beginning to know one another after so many years apart. Would this cause a breach that could never be mended?

"What did my sister say to your proposal?" Spode asked.

Geoffrey blinked. *Bloody hell!* "Ah. She never said as we were interrupted by my children." The way Spode tapped his fingers together didn't bode well, surely. "She didn't say no." Geoffrey thought back. "She seemed interested. She touched my cheek." *Why had he said that?* He didn't like how Spode sat back and stared at him.

"I withdraw my offer, Spode," Wickerdun said as he rose. "I've heard enough."

Geoffrey rose as well, but Ardmoor grabbed his arm and shook his head.

Chapter Four
Lady Emily Must Decide

Emily paced in her bedchamber, awaiting Spode's request for her presence. It was only a matter of time. Her brother would demand an explanation, quite rightfully, too, after what he'd seen. What *everyone* had seen! Emily covered her face with her hands in mortification. She giggled. Oh, how it must have looked. Another giggle, and now a sob.

Had Geoffrey proposed to her? She'd been told he was a great tease, a jokester. Before this morning she'd not believed Maddy and Ardmoor, seeing only a surly and solemn Geoffrey. Had he been serious or making a joke? She groaned. What kind of sister was she, wondering if Geoffrey had proposed to her when Wickerdun was awaiting her answer for his proposal of marriage? Surely Spode expected her to accept Wickerdun. He'd never allow her to wed Geoffrey.

Drat! The image of Geoffrey's grey eyes and his devastating smile kept getting in the way when she tried to picture Wickerdun. Also his...whatever it was, his male part. She'd never forget the hardness, or the sudden knowledge of what it was she was feeling. He'd known when she'd understood. That's when he said he wanted to kiss her. Emily's stomach flipped at the memory. She groaned. How could she possibly—with all due respect and honor—accept Wickerdun's proposal when it was his brother who had invaded her mind, and she feared, her heart?

* * * *

"She may not accept me," Geoffrey said. "Spode might—"

His brother rested a hand on his shoulder. "I believe she will accept you, and I believe Spode will allow her to wed you."

As much as Geoffrey wanted to marry Lady Emily, he didn't want to lose his brother's friendship. "I never expected, or intended, to come between you and Lady Emily. If I could—"

His brother squeezed his shoulder. "Say no more on the subject. When I heard you say she touched your cheek, I knew it was over." Wickerdun gave him a slight smile. "So did Spode. Lady Emily is a fine woman. I shall be pleased to have her as sister-in-law. I shall rejoice at your wedding. Truly."

* * * *

Emily smoothed the skirt of her gown until she could no longer avoid her brother's eyes. She looked up. "I don't want to disappoint you."

Spode exhaled. "That's not what I asked, Em. As for disappointing me, Wickerdun has withdrawn his proposal, so accepting him now is a moot point."

Her smile was immediate, but quickly faded. "Is he very angry? Oh, I don't want to come between you and Wickerdun!" Both hands pressed her chest. "Oh, no! Wickerdun and Geoffrey!"

"Our friendship is strong enough to weather this. Rest assured the brothers have settled it between them. Now, judging by the smile I saw, you weren't going to accept Wickerdun's proposal. So, I ask again, shall I allow Captain DeBohun to court you?"

Emily shifted. "Did he ask for permission?" She breathed a little easier when Spode smiled.

"No, he said he asked you to marry him. But I'd rather go through the formalities if you don't mind."

Emily smiled and nodded her head. "Yes, that would be best."

* * * *

"I think we should go back inside, Em," Geoffrey whispered before nipping her ear lobe. He chuckled when she shivered and clung to him. "Really, we . . ." Well, he couldn't disappoint her if she wanted to kiss him, could he?

"Why can't we run to Gretna Green?" Emily asked after their kiss.

"Well," he said as he leaned his forehead against hers, "one, your brother would have my head, two, my brother would have another part of my anatomy, and three, Ardmoor says he'd teach my children every curse word he knows, including those in Spanish and Portuguese, if I dragged you north and caused another scandal. Fourth, Maddy would lecture me from now until my ears fell off, fifth, the children are looking forward to the wedding, and last but not least, our wedding is tomorrow." He smiled when she laughed.

"The six months have gone by quickly, haven't they?" She looked into his eyes. "Then there are times—"

"Like now when it seems like we'll never be allowed to be together alone—"

"For more than a few minutes—"

He held her closer while glaring at Ardmoor over her head. "Without someone coming to find out where we've taken ourselves to find some privacy."

Ardmoor winked at Geoffrey and silently backed away.

Geoffrey looked down at Emily. "I bless the day Joy met you." His chest swelled at her large smile.

"Don't forget her Christmas wishes."

"Never, my love."

"My dearest love," she replied, tugging on his head and meeting his lips with hers.

The Passage to Summer

Chapter One
The Passage to Summer

"Mark my words, Wickerdun, these next few weeks will bloody well change your life," the Earl of Ardmoor had said. Wickerdun pulled firmly on his beaver hat before urging his horse forward. He didn't feel any different. Two days he'd been at Ardmoor's country estate; regret for his impulsive acceptance of Ardmoor's invitation was all he felt.

"Any man would feel lower than a bloody snake's arse if his prospective bride chose his brother instead of him as husband." Wickerdun *certainly* didn't feel lower than a snake's arse. He was happy for Lady Emily and Geoffrey. Really.

"A new perspective is what you need, Wickerdun. Ride out to the woods—they are enchanted, by the way—and when you see the two old, gnarled oaks that look like sentry points, enter. Ha! You will think you have entered a passage to summer. That is where you need to be, Wickerdun. Remove your coat—bloody hell! Go down to your shirtsleeves and bare feet! Lie on the grass and bray your bloody troubles to the sky. You will be amazed at what happens."

* * * *

Wickerdun found the two gnarled oaks. He shivered as cold rain beat sideways against his face. *A passage to summer?* Ardmoor was doubtless having fun at his expense. He turned his horse to return, but hesitated. Ardmoor wasn't one to make a man look a fool. To reappear and explain to his host that he never entered the wood would seem churlish. Wickerdun turned and rode past the oaks.

He stopped a few feet into the wood, and looked back. Yes, it was dark and raining where he'd come from, yet in the wood . . . He smiled. There was light. There was sunshine! There was warmth. How was this possible? Who cared? After dismounting and tethering his horse, he pulled off his jacket, flung it aside, and sat to remove his boots. He would greatly appreciate all the light and warmth he could get.

Soon Wickerdun lay on the warm, grassy ground with his hands under his head. When was the last time he felt so . . . what was the word? Ah, felt so free? He puckered his brow and lips. *Never?* "Bah! Bah, I say!" he shouted. He smiled at his inanity, closed his eyes, and dreamed.

Pleasant dreams departed. Questions, endless questions. He opened his eyes when he heard singing, only to see an angel staring down at him. No, a faery. Ardmoor said the woods were enchanted, so the vision above him must be a faery. Her eyes were a green-blue, aqua like the sea. Large, lovely eyes. Her lips smiled and he smiled back. The faery laughed and pushed stray strands of blondish hair from her face. *Odd, I would not think faeries pinned back their hair.*

"Hello, good sir."

Aware of his duty as gentleman to rise and apologize for his intrusion, Wickerdun fought years of upbringing. *The woods are enchanted, so I needn't act as I normally would. Besides, she might disappear if I rise.* "Hello. Are you a faery?"

She laughed and the sound made Wickerdun smile. *When was the last time I heard genuinely happy laughter?*

"A faery? No, although the wildness of what some call faery runs through my veins." She cocked her head and looked intently into his eyes. Wickerdun held his breath. Never had a woman looked so keenly at him. "I believe you *also* have a dram or two of that blood running in your veins."

A niggle of memory tapped Wickerdun, but he ignored all but the vision above him. "Do I?"

"Oh, aye." She laughed, then sat back on her heels. "Your presence was noted at once, the subject of much discussion."

Wickerdun thought he might like to hear from her lips what had been said, but not now. "And so you came."

She smiled. "I walk these woods every day. When I heard of your presence, I came to investigate."

Wickerdun's gaze flicked to the trees, from whence he believed the singing came. "The singing . . .?"

"You can hear the wood nymphs?"

The pleasure derived from her bright smile diminished as his mind grappled with her reply. *Wood nymphs? I shall have to ponder that later.* "What is your name?" He frowned when she pulled back. "Forgive me, but I am not familiar with faery custom."

"Courtesy is the same the world over, sir."

I should have known that. I do know that!

She smiled again, and Wickerdun's heart thumped when two dimples appeared on her cheeks. By Jupiter, but she was uncommonly pretty!

"But since we are in the country, in my enchanted wood, perhaps propriety can be eased. My name is Megara. Do you have a name?"

Megara. It suited her. "Wickerdun."

She frowned. "No, your given name. I told you mine."

Wickerdun blinked at such forwardness, then was quick to forgive her. "William." Her one arched brow showed he'd not fooled her. He was impressed. "Clarence William Marshall DeBohun is my name, but I prefer William."

"William." She nodded and smiled. "I like that. What causes you such pain, William?"

"I am not—"

"Oh, but you are." She nodded again, her gaze traveling his body, lingering on his chest before resting on his eyes. He hoped she'd continue to look into his eyes—while remaining silent. "Your body is fairly shrieking with pain. 'Tis most disconcerting to those who can hear."

He chuckled, then caught himself. *By Jupiter! When was the last time I felt like laughing?* "Forgive my shrieking. If I knew how, I would stop."

She crossed her arms and narrowed her eyes. "Ardmoor sent you here."

"How—"

"How is the peg-legged fool these days?"

Wickerdun rose to a sitting position. Enchanting faery she might be, beautiful, dimples, a smile to melt a man's heart, but Ardmoor was a hero and friend. "I believe calling a man a peg-legged fool—"

"I warned him, you know. I told him he would get the thing shot off if he was not careful. He did not listen, did he? The man is a stubborn fool. Always has been, and now has a wooden leg to show for it."

It was but a moment before Wickerdun realized by sitting how close his face was to hers. She had a few freckles on her nose. Odd, but instead of inspiring distaste, he wanted to kiss them. His gaze flew to her eyes when she touched her freckles.

"I apologize if I offended you," she said. "Ardmoor is a dear friend of mine, too."

Wickerdun frowned. "Are you able to read people's minds?" Deuced uncomfortable if she could.

She laughed. "I certainly would not do so without permission. That would be unconscionable. I do have the ability to *see* things, as I did with Ardmoor. The Sight. Not all the time, mind you."

Wickerdun breathed his relief. "And you hear bodies when they shriek."

His breath caught when she winked at him and wagged a finger inches from his face. He overcame the urge to wrap his lips around her finger.

"You are twigging me, William. And yes, I do hear bodies when they scream. One of my abilities. Speaking of which . . . did that hurt? You look surprised."

Wickerdun looked up. She'd pushed him down! What was she about? Would she join him? "I am not hurt, no, but as you say, surprised. What are you planning?"

"To help you, William," she said with a smile.

* * * *

"You looked improved, Wickerdun. Your bloody scowl is gone. Believe I see what could be termed a smile. Found the passage to summer, eh?"

Wickerdun knew his smile was broad. How to describe the freedom experienced, joy at laughing at nothing, at everything, the pleasure in having a beautiful faery listen, enthralled by his every word as if they foretold her future happiness? How to describe all that to a man like Ardmoor? "Yes, I did. Thank you."

* * * *

"I said, Ardmoor is back, Megara."

Megara blinked and set aside her thoughts about this afternoon. William. She wasn't positive, but she believed she'd found her future husband. Time would tell. She sipped her wine and nodded at her aunt. "Yes, I met one of his guests today."

Her aunt raised her brows.

"Wickerdun. Ardmoor sent him to the wood."

"Wickerdun? The Earl of Wickerdun?"

"I believe so. Quite pleasant."

"Is he? Pity you are to marry Shelton."

Megara cleared her throat. "We have not exactly—"

Her aunt tapped her finger on the table before motioning the servants from the room. "Megara, you are four and twenty. Shelton is the *third* man with whom you have formed an understanding. Do *not* tell me he will be the third man to discover you have introduced him to the perfect woman for him!"

"Is it not best to wed the one perfect for you? I speak not only of love, for I realize how fleeting love can be. But what of similar likes and dislikes, opinions, taste in music, travel, food, books?"

"What do you think women friends are for?"

"Remember I can see things, Aunt Susan. Trust me when I say I have seen the future with the three men involved, and what I have seen leaves me near tears. It would kill my soul were I to be bound for life to those men. Good men that they are, they are not meant for me."

Her aunt sat rigid, her lips thinned, her nostrils flaring. Megara waited, not sure the extent of her aunt's displeasure.

"I personally chose those men for you, Megara. Are you saying your ability to see is better than mine?"

"For me, yes." Megara shuddered when her aunt's eyes narrowed.

"I tell you what I see, missy. I see you wed and with child this time next year."

Megara leaned forward. "Who do you see as my husband?" She pulled back at sight of her aunt's sly smile. "Who?"

* * * *

"Check," Ardmoor said.

Wickerdun rubbed his chin and nodded.

"I have you in check, Wickerdun. I bloody well want it acknowledged."

Wickerdun looked up. "Check?" He looked at the board and scowled. "I have not been put in check in years."

Ardmoor laughed. "Doubtless the long conversations with our Lady Meg has your mind turned inside out."

Lady Meg. Wickerdun snorted and shook his head. His extraordinary outburst from earlier today came to mind.

"I have never heard such drivel in my life!" He'd grabbed his clothes and pointed his boot at Megara. "You are but a

child of the forest, a cipher, a faery woman, for God's sake,
who probably reads Mary Shelly!"

"Well, yes, but—"

"I knew it! How dare you insinuate I have no emotions?
Can you not hear me shouting? By Jupiter, I never shout!
Gentlemen do not shout! Good day!"

"You have the right of it. She says the most outrageous
things to me, about me, yet after I have time to reflect, I
realize she is correct."

"She has the Sight. It is in her blood."

"That may be, but how that faery became so wise in
understanding the human nature, I cannot fathom."

Ardmoor leaned forward. "She didn't tell you she was a
bloody faery, did she?"

"No. It is how I think of her. A faery."

Ardmoor nodded. "So you and she are still on speaking
terms?"

Wickerdun laughed aloud. "Yes, we are. But it is a near
thing each and every day. Why do you ask?"

Ardmoor shook his head. "Curious. Never known her to
take such a bleeding interest in someone. Says most men
bore her after the second or third conversation." He winked
at him. "The lady faery must see something about you that
intrigues her."

Ardmoor laughed. "Well, Wickerdun, so after the time
you have spent here, was I right?"

Wickerdun's gaze turned from the game he'd just lost to
Ardmoor and he smiled. "You were right, Ardmoor. This trip
was just what I needed."

"'Course it was. Wouldn't have invited you otherwise.
Changed you for the better."

* * * *

"I love April in the park," Wickerdun said as he lay on the
grass, his head resting on his hands.

"Your park at home? Fairhills?"

"No, Hyde Park in London."

"Oh."

"Do *not* begin questioning me why I am not speaking of my home."

"William! I was clarifying your answer. I know people enjoy the Season in London, and being seen in the park is part of that. I wanted to make sure which park you were referring to. My, but you are quarrelsome today."

Wickerdun turned to face Megara as she sat nearby. He arched a brow. "Insolent faery."

Megara leaned forward and stuck out her tongue before leaning back. "Tell me what you love about April in the park, William. If your description is accurate enough, it will transport the both of us there."

William's lips easily formed a smile. He hadn't known he liked whimsy before meeting Megara. He gazed appreciatively at her, admired her beauty, admired her quicksilver mind and way with words. Her wit he appreciated, but didn't always enjoy; not when it was aimed in his direction. If he could find a woman like Megara to take as wife . . . "Just the two of us?" His gaze traveled to the blue unicorn grazing nearby. He never pictured a unicorn having such a hairy coat. Her laughter caught his attention.

"Yes, the two of us. Ricco might draw unwanted attention."

"Ricco? Sounds rather unusual for a unicorn to be named Ricco."

"Well, he is from Spain."

Wickerdun nodded. Of course.

"So Lady Emily didn't break your heart?"

Wickerdun smiled, more at himself than the question. He lay on the warm grass, eyes closed, listening to the soft song of wood nymphs, enjoying Megara's company. "I daresay Lady Emily wondered if I had a heart. And no to your question, she did not break my heart."

"Of course she knew you had a heart, William," Megara said. "You said throughout your school days you spent every holiday with your friend, Lady Emily's brother, and Lady Emily knew you as well as she knew her own brother. Were you disappointed when she chose your brother to wed?"

Wickerdun turned to glare at Megara. "Obviously I would be disappointed. I believed it was all worked out." He turned his attention back to the leaves in the trees. "Now I have to begin the process of selecting a wife all over again. You have no idea how time consuming, how delicate in nature the inquiries, the—"

"Did you love her?"

Wickerdun laughed shortly, but kept his gaze skyward. "I was fond of her, and I believe she of me. Perhaps in time we would have developed a marital love."

"Sounds rather boring. Like keeping a horse in a fixed trot, never galloping or jumping. Trot, trot, trot."

Wickerdun smiled. "Far safer, my little faery."

"Safer, yes, but . . . Oh, William! Would you settle for trotting the rest of your life?"

The anguish in her voice turned Wickerdun's attention. "I know you mean well, but I am used to trotting." He chuckled at her expression.

"You were born to race, William, not trot!"

* * * *

"Have you seen Wickerdun again?"

Megara turned her attention to her aunt. *You know I have.* "Yes. He's visited the wood daily since his arrival three weeks ago. A remarkable man." She stared past her aunt. "Considering what I have seen of his past, and what he's deemed proper enough to mention, he is a most remarkable man."

"Is he? How long will he be visiting?"

Megara's gaze swung back to her aunt. "You aren't inviting—"

Her aunt waved her question aside. "I extended an invitation to Ardmoor and his guest. That butler of his,

Larkwing, brought back my invitation. It was crumpled into a ball!"

Megara laughed. "Well, Aunt, I told you it would be a long while before Ardmoor forgave you for turning that lovely Andalusian he presented to you into a pretend unicorn. Dyed blue, no less."

* * * *

Megara clutched the letter from cousin Catherine and smiled. She was free once again. William immediately came to mind. Lightly touching him with her mind as he and Ardmoor traveled toward London, she wished him a pleasant, safe journey. As she had ever since meeting him, she resisted the urge to enter and read his mind concerning her. Oh, the strong feelings would slip by, and those she grabbed. She knew he admired her, and had manly, physical thoughts concerning her. But every male had those ideas about any woman who passed their sight. No, William had wanted to kiss her freckles. That was so sweet. No man, ever, had wanted to kiss her freckles.

She frowned. William was headed for London. In search of a wife. Suppose he found one before she arrived? Which was likely after all their conversations. He hadn't revealed all his past to her, so she hadn't been able to talk to him about that. She wasn't at ease over those memories he kept so tightly bound. But unless he brought them up first, she had to remain silent. On a positive note, the man finally began to see he didn't have to turn into his father, something that had kept him closed to all the world had to offer. Realizing he could decide his own future, William had begun to open, blossoming as it were, like a manly flower. He was uncommonly handsome, too. Dark hair and grey eyes she'd stared into whenever she had the chance. Down to the bone polite. Intelligent, considerate. Lord! She'd done too good a job. She had to get there and begin her pursuit before some other woman snatched him away from her!

* * * *

"Lady Catherine is to wed Shelton? Your cousin, Catherine?"

"Yes, Aunt."

Megara ignored her aunt's flaring nostrils and waved the letter announcing the betrothal. "I believe they will be most happy with one another."

"The girl has a gap as wide as the channel between her front teeth!"

"Which Shelton found irresistible. What's done is done, Aunt. Shelton and Catherine will be quite happy, I assure you, else I would not have introduced them to each other. And my brother did say the final decision concerning marriage was to be mine. So . . ." She tossed aside the letter and cleared her throat. "I have reconsidered. I believe I would enjoy a Season in London. Being presented. Balls. Going to Hyde Park and being seen. Assemblies and such. Why are you frowning? You did say an earl's daughter should do these things."

"Six years ago!"

"I have changed my mind. Six years ago I knew it would come to naught."

"What has changed?"

Megara smiled as the image of William came to mind. "I have met the man for me and he will be in London."

"Wickerdun, eh? Not surprised. Why did you not snap him up while he was here?"

"Because I was not free to do so. Now that Shelton and Catherine are engaged, I am free. Unless you have arranged another understanding on my behalf?"

Her aunt shook her head.

"Why are you frowning? What do you see?"

"This is such short notice, Meg. 'Tis already March. You will need an entire wardrobe of new clothes, and that takes time. I shall have to contact my friends when we arrive, and see who—"

"I shall write to Maddy, Ardmoor's sister. She is now Countess of Spode. Doubtless she will be able to aid me." *Undoubtedly the best person in London to aid me since she's married to William's oldest friend.*

Chapter Two
To London

Wickerdun wasn't sure how much longer he could keep smiling. The mindless drivel, boring monologues, and vicious gossip were near driving him mad. How had he endured all this in past Seasons? Another simpering laugh or bored sigh and he was sure he'd snap. It was all her fault. Megara.

All was fine upon his arrival in London, three weeks ago. He felt renewed, in body, mind and spirit. Looked forward to the coming Season. Seeing Lady Emily and his brother Geoffrey hadn't bothered him in the slightest. In fact, he was now completely convinced Lady Emily had chosen the proper man. She wasn't right for him at all, but perfect for his brother. With that settled in his mind, he was ready, nay, eager, to find a wife.

It began in the park. It was April, the sun was shining, and people were out, riding and walking. He'd so looked forward to his first ride. He planned to re-create what he'd described to Megara. He had, but it didn't soothe him, didn't bring him the satisfaction he expected. He wasn't pleased. Neither did he find enjoyment in the Season's consequent entertainments. As he met the debutantes and renewed his acquaintance with ladies available for matrimony, he mentally crossed each off his list. None measured up to Megara. His outlook had changed, and with that, unfortunately, everything had changed.

He noticed the singing two weeks ago when he was in the park, singing that sounded suspiciously like wood nymphs.

Then he kept thinking he saw Meg. Was he going insane? Had Megara placed some sort of faery curse on him?

* * * *

"Nonsense, I am delighted to help you!" Maddy, the Countess of Spode said.

Megara breathed a sigh of relief. "Good, for I had not realized when Aunt Susan said country manners wouldn't do for London that I would be so restricted in my efforts! How *does* a woman indicate her desire to be pursued without appearing to be a strumpet?"

"Well . . ."

"I have seen him in the park, but Aunt Susan absolutely refused to allow me to initiate a conversation. She says she must be introduced to him first, and then I may speak to him. Really, I never had such problems in the country."

Maddy laughed. "The country is more relaxed, but then, everyone knows everyone, do they not? I shall have my husband introduce Wickerdun to your aunt. That should suit. I am surprised Wickerdun did not acknowledge you by a nod, at the very least. Ardmoor said he was quite taken with you."

Megara grinned and fanned her face. "I was much taken by him. As to his acknowledging me, he always looked a bit shocked when he saw me, as if he was not sure it was really me." Megara inched forward. "Do you happen to know if I have any competition? I so hate to disappoint someone, but William and I are destined to be together."

"You saw this?"

"When my Sight works, I can see for anyone. Yet when it comes to myself, I cannot see far. I feel William and I are a suitable match, although my aunt says I have a difficult time ahead of me." Megara wrinkled her nose. "I think she said that just to twig me."

* * * *

Wickerdun halted and stared across the room. When his view was obstructed by people he moved to look again, sure the vision of his faery would be gone. But no, she was still there. Gowned as befitted an heiress, in something gold that flowed over her body, and with a large plume in her hair. She was magnificent. *Who was she?* She could be Megara's double in appearance, but would she have Megara's personality? It would be too much to hope she would have freckles. Ladies did not permit freckles to mar their complexion.

His breath caught when she turned and smiled at him. *Please, oh please . . . let that be a sign she's the one.* He smiled when he saw Spode and his wife beside his vision. Good, he'd be able to get an introduction.

He kept his eyes on the woman as he approached. His steps slowed. The closer he drew near, the stronger the feeling of unreality. She couldn't be Megara. Megara was a strange, wild and free faery who walked the forest and passage to summer. She was friendly with blue, shaggy unicorns. Wood nymphs sang for her pleasure. He'd confided in her because it was safe, because she was a faery. By Jupiter, he'd removed his clothing in front of her! This couldn't be Megara!

He kept his eyes on the woman even when Spode and his wife turned to him. He knew before he heard the introduction it was Megara when she smiled at him. *Lady Megara Ivers, sister to the Earl of Blackhyrst.* Only when he was introduced to her aunt did he speak, the practiced words coming out effortlessly. Before anyone spoke, he bowed and excused himself.

"Zounds!" Spode exclaimed as he stared after his friend.

* * * *

"Oh, dear!" Maddy said.

"That is the man you are set to wed?" Aunt Susan asked.

Megara stared after William, her welcoming smile slowly fading. Why had he been so angry? Anger and . . . what was the other emotion she'd caught? Betrayal? She slowly shook her head. *What* convoluted notions were wending their way through that man's brain?

* * * *

"I am waiting, Ardmoor," Wickerdun said the next morning. After storming into Ardmoor's study, he trusted his clipped words conveyed his vast disgruntlement

"You can bloody well wait until I have the right of this, Wickerdun. I would say you were foxed except you are not a man to indulge this early in the day. Neither do you appear to have been up all night. Never heard any talk of you jumping off the course, you are unfailingly polite to the point you would slit your own throat before uttering a derogatory word, and I would swear you to be the kind of man who explores every possible ramification before opening his mouth. Therefore, I am bloody well confused about what I have to apologize for."

Having surmised he'd been the object of a grand bit of sport, Wickerdun had been keen to demand satisfaction. He couldn't very well challenge Lady Megara. Ardmoor was the obvious target, since he was the one who'd suggested he travel to the wood. But Ardmoor was a war hero, and missing part of his right leg. He couldn't demand satisfaction from the man. But he could *bloody* well demand an apology.

Wickerdun's eyes swung to Ardmoor's bouncing leg. "Will you stop jiggling that beribboned peg? The fluttering is distracting." He nodded briefly when the movement ceased. "I told you, I saw Megara last night, *Lady Megara Ivers*. It was she, Megara from the enchanted wood!" Wickerdun waited, his lips thinning the longer he waited. "Well? What have you to say?"

Ardmoor blew out a breath and shook his head. "I am waiting to hear something of importance. Maddy mentioned

Meg and her aunt had come to town. Did she insult you? Give you the cut? What?"

Wickerdun ran a finger under his cravat. "No, no! She said not a word. She smiled at me!"

Ardmoor chuckled.

"Ah ha! You think it is funny! A grand jest at my expense. Tell me, has everyone heard how the Earl of Wickerdun fell under the spell of the faery Megara?" Ardmoor's incredulous expression gave Wickerdun a moment's pause.

"The faery . . .? You truly believed Megara was a bloody faery?"

Wickerdun pursed his lips and raised his gaze to the ceiling. "What else was I to believe?"

"I asked you if she told you she was a faery, and you said no. Why should . . .?"

Wickerdun sat heavily across from Ardmoor. "Why? An enchanted wood? *Her* enchanted wood, she said. Passage to summer? The songs of wood nymphs, which, by the way, I am starting to hear again! Oh, and let us not forget the shaggy, blue unicorn! And you ask why I might think she is a faery? My God, Ardmoor! I undressed down to my shirt and breeches before her!"

"Ah," Ardmoor said and sat back. "Wickerdun . . . the shaggy blue unicorn is a horse. A bloody expensive horse. A gift from me to Meg's aunt. An Andalusian. The old bat dyes it blue and attaches a horn. I gather you did not have a close look."

Wickerdun let himself slump. "No. Meg, er, Lady Megara said it was not safe to approach."

"Because it bloody well hates the bloody horn attached to its bloody face!"

Wickerdun sat back and closed his eyes. "I suppose you have a logical explanation for everything?" He snorted when Ardmoor grinned. "Very well. Explain for me please."

Wickerdun swirled his brandy while Ardmoor spoke. Finally he cut in. "I shall accept the hot springs theory because nothing else makes sense, although I truly doubt it would account for the summer-like weather. I *do* recall you said the Earl of Blackhyrst's estate was near yours, so when Lady Megara said the wood was hers, she meant her family. I do have difficulty accepting the fact that wood nymphs exist, let alone they sing to please Lady Megara."

"No, you misunderstood me, Wickerdun. Wood nymphs sing all the bleeding time. One cannot get away from their bloody, chirpy voices if you are near a wood. Our Meg is appreciative and tells them so. Therefore, when she is near, they make sure she hears their song. That is why you have started hearing them again. Because Lady Megara has come to town."

Wickerdun stared. "You expect me to believe that?"

"You bloody well hear them, do you not?"

"But wood nymphs do not exist!"

Ardmoor arched his brows. "Do they not? Then why do you hear singing, Wickerdun? You have attics to let, do you?"

Wickerdun stared at his snifter and then swallowed. "Why me? Why now?"

Ardmoor shrugged. "I expect it is due to your blood. As for why now, I surmise it is due to the fact Lady Megara showed you how to view things differently."

"What do you mean, my blood?" He drew his brows together. "You said that before, did you not? Concerning Joy's wish and my brother . . . Lady Megara also said I had some of . . ." A silly topic. His eyes narrowed. "Do you hear the wood nymphs, too?"

Ardmoor grimaced. "All the bleeding time. It is our wild blood, don't you know. The Ivers, though, they hail back to Eric Ivarsson who married a truly wild-blooded woman. That blood passed down through the generations, and when an Ivers female married into the Wilde's, it passed into our family."

"You are related to her family?"

Ardmoor leaned forward to slap his knee. "You would be surprised how many people have the wild blood. Makes them a bit different. Special."

Wickerdun nodded and held out his glass. The two men drank quietly together until Wickerdun rose. "I have to offer for her."

Ardmoor nodded. "I can see that."

Wickerdun closed his eyes and shuddered. *Good God, what kind of family am I marrying into? I am done for. After we are wed, we shall have to retire to the country.*

"You look—pardon my blunt words—like a tired, old whore about to take on fifty sailors."

Wickerdun didn't reply.

"If it is any consolation, I do not think she will refuse you. Seems to have set her cap for you."

* * * *

"You what?" Maddy exclaimed.

Ardmoor caught the biscuit, but missed the spoon. It hit him in his chest. "Aim is off, Maddy. You used—" He ducked, the cup missing his head. "Better. What has you so exercised?"

"You told Wickerdun that Meg came to London to marry him!"

"No, but it comes down to that, does it not? It is perfect."

His sister laughed sarcastically. "Given he feels honor bound to offer for her, and being told that is what she intended in the first place, how do you think that makes him feel?"

Ardmoor smiled. "Lower than a snake's belly, I would imagine. As I'd said, it is perfect."

His sister raised her brows. "Oh?"

He leaned forward. "Has Meg ever had anything denied her? Yes, Meg is a sweet girl. But she has never had to work for anything has she? She . . ."—he thrummed his fingers in the air—"she manipulates things her way. Meg has never wanted a man before, has she? Well, she will have to bl— work to get him if she wants Wickerdun."

Maddy issued a soft snort. "Meg is more than you know, Ardmoor. She cares about people. And I certainly hope Wickerdun has more sense than to approach her with a proposal of marriage due to an inane belief he compromised her!"

* * * *

Wickerdun was relieved Lady Megara resided in Mayfair. The house was in good repair, impressive in fact. Why hadn't he met her before? Surely they would have crossed paths in past Seasons? The abundance of trees near the house gave Wickerdun pause. The low murmur of singing changed to loud song when he approached the house, bursting into maniacal happiness when he started up the steps. He fairly flung himself inside to escape when the butler informed him Lady Megara was receiving.

Wickerdun took himself in hand and followed the servant to the drawing room. The singing of wood nymphs, while annoying, was not important when viewed with the reason for his visit. Namely, he was here to propose to Lady Megara, set the date, and allow her time to prepare her trousseau. They would wed, and if—a large *if*—he was satisfied she'd not be an embarrassment to him, they would remain in London while Parliament sat. She could be taught how to be a proper hostess. If not, they would retire to . . .

Wickerdun closed his eyes. No, he couldn't return there. Not with her.

* * * *

Megara looked up when William entered. His colors were not good, dark and holding close to his body. "Welcome, my lord." She smiled and turned back to Mr. Shields. "You were saying, Mr. Shields?"

"Do you really see Lady Delphine as my future wife? For I have had thoughts in that direction, but she is always surrounded by other men. Didn't see as I would have a chance. Well, being the third son and all."

Megara smiled. "My lord, of course she is always surrounded by other men! She is a delightful creature who exudes nothing but happiness and good will. Who would not want to be near such a person? But I assure you, Lady Delphine seeks a husband such as you. Because of her dowry, she has the freedom to accept or refuse as it pleases her, which, in a perfect world, would be best for all of us, would it not? A man such as yourself, a man from good family, sensible, good health and pleasing appearance, oh yes, she watches you! Tonight, put forth yourself. Speak to her from your heart and you'll not be disappointed."

* * * *

William stood while Lady Megara spoke with her callers, awaiting his turn. He hoped he hid his surprise upon seeing her drawing room filled with flowers and suitors. Obviously, Megara, *Lady* Megara, had a successful evening. But *what* the devil was she saying that kept each man riveted to her every word? He closed his eyes and hoped it wouldn't come back and haunt them. He snapped open his eyes. Spode was a stickler. If there was any hint of derogatory talk concerning Lady Megara, he'd not have introduced her. Wickerdun breathed a sigh of relief. Of course, Ardmoor had said the Wilde's and the Ivers were related. Since his wife was a Wilde, might Spode have felt obligated to introduce Lady Megara? No, he didn't think so.

What the devil was taking so long? Why did each fellow quietly wait his turn? He'd never attended a morning visit such as this. Mentally rehearsing his speech, Wickerdun didn't feel quite so desperate. The marriage might work out. She acted quite normal, in fact. He tipped his head and studied her. A vision of loveliness, one that had stepped off a fashion plate. Not that he knew the latest fashions, but she was certainly gowned as other women who always wore the latest and most fashionable styles. What might be her preference for jewelry? Emeralds? He'd enjoy seeing her wear something he chose for her. Which brought Ella to mind. Should he give her something extra, aside from a good settlement, when she was given her *conge?* Wickerdun knew it was expected he'd retain his mistress after his marriage. Yet, that, he couldn't do. Not only was it reminiscent of his father, but the thought of sleeping with Ella and then his wife did not agree with Wickerdun. Once wed, he intended to be faithful.

The room cleared sufficiently that a chair became available. Unfortunately, it placed him next to her aunt. He'd forgotten about the aunt who dyed horses blue and attached horns to their heads. Surely, there would be talk about her. Of course, *he'd* never heard any talk about the Ivers, had he? With that cheering thought, Wickerdun turned and smiled at the aunt. She arched her brow, and he turned his gaze toward Lady Megara, but he could feel the aunt's stare.

"Lady Megara appears quite popular," he said. When he turned, the aunt nodded and picked up her needlework.

"My niece is popular wherever she goes. It is just getting her to go that is the very devil." She looked at him. "She is stubborn and thinks she knows best. Well, I shall allow she's gifted."

Wickerdun opened his mouth to reply, but had no idea what to say. "She is a quick wit." The aunt gave a small laugh in reply.

"How do you like it?" she asked as she thrust her needlework toward him.

He recognized Ricco, standing in the wood, his head held high. *How on earth did the woman keep the horn attached? Surely the horse would try to rub it off?* A question for another time.

Wickerdun pursed his lips and nodded. "You are most gifted, my lady. The shades of blue most artistically stitched."

The aunt smiled and pressed the cloth against her lap. "It is Ricco. I understand you saw him in the wood one day."

He gripped the chair arms and nodded.

"What did you think?"

His gaze swung to Megara. He was next! Would the aunt live with them after they wed? He turned to her. "Well, I was surprised by the shagginess, I must confess. And the blue color." He shifted slightly when she didn't reply, but cocked her head to study him. "I hope I have not offended you."

Her gaze sharpened with that. "You are nothing like your father, boy. You can be grateful for that." She glanced toward Megara, then back at him. "My niece is awaiting your company."

* * * *

When William approached Megara, his colors were swirling. "Has conversing with my aunt confounded you? She likes to do that, you know." She patted the chair next to her. "Would you care for—"

"Why have I not met you before?" he asked as he sat.

Poor William. Megara smiled in amusement at his shocked expression.

He shook his head as if to clear it. "That is not what I meant to say."

"Well, it is a good question. I could ask the same of you."

He opened his mouth as if to speak, but closed it.

"My lord, perhaps it was not the right time for us to meet. Perhaps if we had met years ago, we would not have appreciated the other as the unique person they are." She shrugged. "Everything in its own time."

"But I have attended each Season for years. I find it most—"

"Oh, but this is my first Season, my lord." He looked at her blankly. "You see, I never wanted a Season, for I knew it would be pointless, since the man I would marry would not be present." She leaned forward when he winced. "Are you in pain, my lord?"

"No. Please go on."

"Meg, my love, time to say goodbye to Wickerdun," her aunt interrupted. "You must rest and prepare for tonight's entertainments."

Wickerdun rose at the woman's words, bade his farewell and headed outside. Out in the street, he placed his hat firmly on his head, barely noting the singing wood nymphs. He looked back at the house. What the devil happened in there? He'd meant to propose to her. And what the devil did she mean her future husband hadn't been present in London all those prior Seasons before? How could she know that? Did that mean she knows her future husband is now present? The devil!

* * * *

Later that evening, William struggled to converse with Megara during the dance. He should have chosen a waltz when he marked her dance card.

"Why the . . . why did you not tell me who you were?"

Her eyes widened before crinkling in silent laughter. He gritted his teeth when the movement of the dance called her away.

"I did," she replied as soon as she returned, clapping her hands against his and revolving.

"No, you did not. I had no idea you were Lady Megara Ivers." He growled when the dance steps separated them.

"Would that have made a difference?" she asked upon her reappearance. "Would you have spoken with such honesty if you thought me a peeress instead of a country girl?"

"Ha! I thought you some enchanted creature, not a farm girl." He caught himself from stumbling when she smiled at him.

"You thought I was an enchanted creature? How sweetly expressed."

He watched in resignation as she skipped away to her new partner. His new partner's determined efforts to converse foiled his plan to prepare for Lady Megara's return.

"I thought our conversations and time together were enchanting as well," she said as soon as she returned. "If I may be so bold as to say such a thing."

"That is exactly my point! The fact that I . . ." When she curtsied, he realized the dance was ended. "We need to talk, Lady Megara." His stomach sank when she shook her head and showed him her filled dance card. "What about supper? Perhaps we—"

"You should have marked the supper dance, Wickerdun. Is it not silly the *ton* believes a man cannot dance more than twice with a woman? Although I believe we could converse as you escort me back to my aunt."

Wickerdun ran his hands through his hair. "Tomorrow then. We shall ride together in the park."

* * * *

"Don't believe I have ever seen Wickerdun in such a state," Spode said. He grinned at his wife and brother-in-law. "Good to see the man falling so hard."

"Who is falling?" Lady Emily asked as she and Geoffrey, Wickerdun's brother, arrived.

"Wickerdun."

The new arrivals turned to see Wickerdun staring into the crowd, his expression one of bewilderment. "But who . . .?"

"Lady Megara Ivers," Ardmoor said. "The Earl of Blackhyrst's estate borders mine. We are distantly related. They met when he came to visit me."

Lady Emily and Geoffrey looked at one another, then at Ardmoor. "What is she like?" Lady Emily asked.

"Is it wise for my brother to form an attachment at this time?" Geoffrey asked.

"Lady Megara is a wonderful woman, perfect for Wickerdun," Maddy assured her sister-in-law.

"In truth, she is just what he needs," Ardmoor said. "Surely you have noted the change in him since his arrival back in London? All due to Lady Megara."

"I have noted his lack of concentration and shortness of temper," Geoffrey replied. "All due to that woman, you say?"

"That woman," Ardmoor said, "has brought your brother to life. Before, the man was so unfailingly pleasant, one wondered if, should he annoy one sufficiently that one might have no choice but plant him a facer to see if he would react, he would apologize for having his nose in the way of your fist!"

* * * *

"The thing is, Lady Megara," Wickerdun said as he slowed his curricle, "I did not know who you were when we talked . . . in the enchanted wood. I believe I thought you were some faery-type creature."

"Oh, William!" She covered her mouth and laughed. "Forgive me, we are no longer in the country. Is that why you looked so shocked the other night?"

"Yes, well, as I was saying, if I *had* known you were a lady rather than the faery I believed, I never would have—"

"Wickerdun, forgive me, but if you are honest with yourself, you knew I was no faery creature. That you did not realize I was Lady Megara Ivers I can believe. But really, how many faeries of your acquaintance wear half boots? Gowns? Hats?"

Wickerdun frowned. Yes, she had worn normal clothes. Old clothes, though. *Had* he always known she was human?

Megara stared at William as he considered her words. "You have dark colors hovering close to your chest."

Whatever did she mean? "Dark colors?"

"Colors change with your mood. For instance, the other night, your colors lightened and swirled about you. You felt happiness instead of the anger and betrayal I first saw in the woods."

"So you are saying my mood today is dark?"

She nodded, as if what she said made perfect sense. "You brood about things that cannot be helped."

In truth, he was brooding, and her perception unnerved him. He pulled the curricle out of the park traffic and stopped.

She smiled in anticipation. "Are we going to walk the paths?"

"No, I . . . Lady Megara, I apologize for my behavior in the wood. I compromised your honor."

"Did you? May I ask when?"

"In the wood, when I removed my clothing."

Megara turned to meet his gaze. "Although you may be overcome with remorse, I must confess I am puzzled by such emotion. Yes, you removed your coat, your waistcoat, your stockings and your boots. We were in the country, where such occurrences do happen. Many things are done in the country that are considered improper in town. So!" She grinned at him. "If that is why you have been so glum, be done with it!" She leaned close and wiggled her brows. "Had you ever visited your country estates, you might have known that." She frowned when he pressed his lips together.

"Lady Megara, I feel honor bound to—"

"Wickerdun," Megara broke in, "if you are going to propose to me, I beg you reconsider. Not that I am averse to such a proposal, mind you. However, if you propose merely because you believe you compromised my honor, and your sense of decency commands you act thusly, then you insult me. I would then become quite cross."

She would be cross if he asked for her hand in marriage? He looked ahead in silence, for how should he respond? Did she or didn't she welcome his proposal?

"Quite a conundrum for a gentleman, is it not?" she said.

* * * *

Wickerdun's gaze fastened on Megara twirling gracefully to a waltz. Seeing her in the arms of another man made his gut clench, his hands itch to fell the man with a hard blow. No, he'd like to pummel the man into the ground, and then drag Megara off to . . . What the devil was wrong with him? He'd never had such violence of feeling, certainly never concerning a woman. What had she done to him? Three days he'd brooded over her reply. He didn't know what she wanted. Hadn't she hinted she'd welcome his proposal? Yet said she'd be cross if he asked for her hand in marriage. What did the reason matter? They would be wed, wouldn't they? He rubbed the back of his neck. He couldn't continue like this. He rued the day he met her, yet he blessed the day he first saw her. The next dance was his. He made a bee-line for her aunt.

For the first two minutes of the waltz, Wickerdun remained silent, content to hold Megara, allowing his mind to wander where he knew they shouldn't, not when the evidence of his thoughts would be visible. His carnal thoughts of lust, although strongly felt, were but part of a belief he was holding the other part of himself; that holding her made him complete.

What a concept. He should flee, get as far away from Lady Megara Ivers as possible. Except he couldn't. He wanted her as his wife, but without the messy emotional part she would be sure to bring along. Of course, that was assuming she'd accept him. Yet, Ardmoor insisted she would. Which reminded him of his decision.

"Lady Megara," he began softly, "may I ask if the man you believe you shall marry is in London?" When she looked up at him, her eyes were softly focused, as if she'd just awakened. It was all he could do to refrain from pulling her into a crushing embrace.

"Not always," she replied.

Wickerdun clenched his jaw and pulled her tighter. Well, that meant it wasn't he. He hadn't left London. Didn't plan to.

"Sometimes I glimpse him, before he retreats."

Wickerdun frowned. What the devil? "He retreats? I do not understand."

"I think you do," she said.

Wickerdun looked down at her face, focusing on her lips. "Come with me." He escorted her off the dance floor. The balcony doors beckoned, much closer than skirting around the dance floor and being stopped for mindless chatter. The balcony would be dark, too.

Wickerdun shook his head. He'd never led a woman onto a darkened balcony. What did she do to him? "You make me forget myself."

"I—"

His lips touched Megara's. Softly, gently. He wanted to drag her to the ground, have his way with her, make her his. A heretofore-unheard part of him reared his shaggy head and said that was exactly what he should do, have done with all the pretty pussy-footing around, grab the mate of his choice, and run. He groaned, refusing to listen, and kept kissing Megara. There was a hazily formed hope she might like kissing him so much she'd agree to marry him.

* * * *

Surely the only reason Megara hadn't melted into a heated pool at William's feet was because he was holding her so tightly. Why hadn't anyone told her how wonderful kissing was? Then he pulled away and spoke to her.

"Marry me, Lady Megara."

She blinked and grabbed onto his arms for support. Yes, she wanted to marry him. She smiled, opened her mouth to say yes, but instead took a woozy step back. "Has your reason changed?"

"What? My reason?" He looked at her blankly. "I want you as my wife. Is that not reason enough?"

Megara frowned and took another step away from him, his presence interfering with her ability to think clearly. "With anyone else, yes. But I want you to race with me, William, not trot through our married life. Are you prepared to race with me?" Even though he frowned as if he didn't understand, Megara wasn't fooled. "You must accept who you are William, and who I am. Accept that you determine your destiny, that your married life does not have to mirror that of your parents."

"I realize that!" he snapped. He took a step closer. "Will you or will you not accept my proposal of marriage?"

"Where would we reside?" Her heart fell when he looked away.

"London, of course. I take my duties in parliament seriously."

"Which is laudable. But where would we live when parliament is not in session?" She tried to catch his gaze.

"I have numerous estates. You may take your pick. Does that answer suffice?"

She shook her head. "Fairhills, William. If you want to race, if you want me to marry you, you need to return to Fairhills." Her heart sank further at his expression.

"We had best return," he said, "before any gossip is started."

* * * *

"You need not do this," Geoffrey said, looking up from the deed gifted to him. "Really, I have done well for myself, for my children. You need not—"

"Allow me this small thing, Geoffrey," Wickerdun said. "I cannot touch the entailed properties—and Father made sure nearly all were entailed. He hated the fact you married Lady Laurel, you know. He wanted to punish you for that. Went out of his way to ensure you would never be accepted by society, let alone live in the bosom of your family. That is why I want you to have this property." He smiled. "Look closely at the deed." Wickerdun's smile increased when his brother looked up with a grin.

"So you managed to acquire the property Father never could? Are you sure? This property edges into the middle of Fairhills. Well, of course you know that. But do you not . . .?"

"I cannot think of a better use for the property, Geoffrey. We were estranged for too long. It would please me to know you and your family were near." Wickerdun's heart raced and stomach turned at the thought of visiting Fairhills. To live there again.

His brother smiled at him. "Emily will be pleased, Wickerdun. So am I. Yes, I accept your wedding present, brother. May our families grow large and strong and happy once again."

Wickerdun shook his head, aware his brother had spoken. "I beg your pardon?"

"I asked when we might expect to see an announcement in *The Times* concerning you and Lady Megara? Ardmoor says had he not been on the lookout the other night, you and the lady in question would have been facing a scandal. Something about being on a darkened balcony for an extended amount of time."

Wickerdun leaned back and pursed his lips. He wasn't sure if he wanted to thank Ardmoor or not. He and Megara might now be engaged. Which told him volumes about his current mental state; never would he consider coercing a woman into marriage with threat of scandal. Of course, this was Megara, so the coercing would doubtless fail in any case.

"For what it is worth, I approve your choice. She will keep you on your toes, too. Just what you need."

Wickerdun grunted. "Yes, she will. Provided she ever accepts my proposal of marriage."

* * * *

"Isn't going back to his home what you wanted him to do?" Maddy asked.

"I *thought* we might go together," Megara answered. "I am not sure he will be able to put all the pieces together by himself. If he cannot, he will be frustrated and remain blind to what went on, even more entrenched in his beliefs and attitudes. He will trot forever."

"I do not think you give Wickerdun enough credit, Meg."

"His mother was a Bruin. Their wild blood ranks near the Ivers." She leaned closer. "His father's family had a mixture of wild blood as well. Unfortunately, his father could not handle the wildness, and became one of those people driven to rages by his inner demons. The man eventually became a twisted, vicious, vengeful soul. William, his brother Geoffrey, and their two sisters have a generous and possibly unstable mixture of old, wild blood. As a child and young boy, William witnessed his father slowly destroy his mother, not by physical force, but by accusations, fits of rage, and the insidious, always present but unexpressed overpowering emotions of shame and fear because she was different. William *felt* it. William felt what his father felt, felt what it was doing to his mother. The boy William learned his lesson; do not express what comes naturally, or you will be beaten into the ground."

"So that is why Wickerdun always chose to spend his holidays with my husband's family," Maddy said. "That explains so much about him. Hmmm, it also explains why Geoffrey is drawn to women with the wild blood. First my sister Laurel, and now Emily."

Megara nodded in agreement. "The thing is, William does not remember all of this." Megara's face grew warm at Maddy's raised brows. "Do not look at me like that, Maddy. I admit I should not have done it, but I peeked a bit. However only when a thought came out to me. Naturally, I had to follow the trail. The man has carefully tucked away early memories of his gifts, as well as those of his mother. He remembers her as a sweet, but weak and sickly woman." Megara sighed. "I am not sure how he will handle his visit to where it all began. I do wish he had thought to invite me along as well."

"You know very well it would be highly improper for you to travel with Wickerdun to his home without a proper escort."

"I do not suppose you would—"

"No, our first ball of the season is next week, so I cannot assist you. Besides, Wickerdun assured Spode he would return in time for the ball."

"Yes, but what kind of shape will he be in, I wonder?"

Chapter Three
Where It Began

Wickerdun handed the reins to the groom and stood staring at the front of Fairhills. It had been years since he voluntarily visited. The house appeared smaller than he remembered. If one didn't have dark memories about the place, one might call the house appealing. Would Megara like it? He looked around, wondering where to start. So many memories, so many ghosts to get rid of. Doubtless, he'd wind up losing his mind over this. He paused as the hint of song drifted to his ear. He smiled. Yes, the song of wood nymphs was just what he needed, actually.

After walking inside, Wickerdun stood in the middle of the drawing room, staring out a window at the bench placed near the rose garden. He pictured his mother sitting there, he running to her with a bloodied knee, crying, and she placing her hand over his scrape. They both laughed when she removed her hand and the wound was healed. She'd said something about blood. Blood all gone?

The soft clearing of a throat behind him was a welcome distraction. He turned. "Yes, Thomas?"

"The coach arrived, my lord, with Jenkins and your bags. He is seeing to your unpacking."

The old butler failed to disguise his curiosity. No doubt the entire staff wondered about Wickerdun's sudden arrival. "Yes, Thomas?"

"Forgive me, my lord, but it appears you'll not be staying long?"

"Just long enough, Thomas." He cast a thoughtful look at the old servant. "You have been at Fairhills all your life, have you not?"

"Yes, my lord. But if you'll forgive me, I'm not ready to be pensioned off."

"Yes, I know. You refuse each time it is offered. No, what I meant was you are familiar with this family."

"It was my honor to begin service under your great-grandfather, sir. A very gifted man, if you will pardon my saying so."

Wickerdun arched his brows. It appeared Thomas might have a wealth of information. "Please have a seat, Thomas. I have many questions about my family, and I believe we shall both be more at ease if we can converse comfortably." Not to mention Thomas looked ready to fall on his face. He really would have to pension the old man off, if only for his own good.

Once they were seated, Wickerdun asked Thomas about his mother.

"There was naught wrong with her, my lord. A wonderful lady. She was most gifted."

Wickerdun drew his brows together. "No, I mean physically wrong with her."

Thomas shook his head. "There was naught wrong with your mother, my lord."

Wickerdun sighed. "My father?" His lips quirked when Thomas drew himself up.

"I never speak ill of the dead, my lord. However, if I might be so bold as to say so, Mrs. Littlepond has no such compunction."

His interest piqued, Wickerdun made a mental note to speak to the housekeeper. "Then tell me about my great-grandfather and grandfather, Thomas."

* * * *

Wickerdun lay in his bed that night, the earlier conversations held with Thomas and Mrs. Littlepond running through his head. A window was open, allowing in the soft, soothing voices of wood nymphs. The singing failed to comfort him, however. The two servants' versions of events past didn't agree with his memories. But, he had to admit, there was much of his childhood he didn't recall.

Gifted. They had both used the word *gifted* when speaking of his mother. Actually, with his entire family, his father the exception. Mrs. Littlepond didn't come out and say his father was responsible for his mother's death, but it was implied. Doubtless they wished to spare his feelings, but he would rather hear the truth, not vague mumblings, heavy sighs and averted gazes.

His announcement of a possible marriage in the near future visibly cheered the two. They asked if his future countess was gifted, too. What an odd thing to ask. He said they would have to determine such a thing for themselves, although it had been Megara who insisted he return to Fairhills. Apparently, she decided this was where they would reside when not in London. Thomas was so excited, Wickerdun feared the man might have an apoplectic attack.

So strange. The visit hadn't been the nightmare he feared, not at all. Yet he still had questions that needed answering. The blood. His mother and his scraped knee. There had been other times when she'd healed his cuts. Geoffrey's, too. The memories flowed. He remembered her talking to him, could see her smile, then point and explain something, but he couldn't recall conversations. So frustrating!

Hours later, the night terror left Wickerdun shaking with residual fear, his body wet with sweat, his heart racing. His father's presence was palpable. *Was the bloody bedchamber haunted?* Gradually, his heart quieted, the rational part of him searching for a reason for his terror. The room slowly brightened as the dawn broke while he lay in bed, thinking.

* * * *

"The thing is," Wickerdun said aloud as he lay on the ground in the wood, "I am not sure my conclusions are correct. This is not something one can discuss with just anyone." He listened to the chatter and singing in reply. "Although I cannot understand what you are saying, I appreciate your harkening. Would you agree I am on the right path? Or am I headed for Bedlam?" More chatter and singing. "Some might call me insane. Some said my father was insane, at the end. Very possibly he was. Then, too, I am having a conversation with wood nymphs, which most people would consider insane, especially since I cannot understand what you are saying. But Ardmoor can hear you. Megara can hear you. So at least I am not the only one." He sighed.

"They would listen and not think me insane, but I would have to travel to London to speak to them and I do not believe it wise for me to leave just yet. I think there is more for me to uncover here." He listened to the loud chattering. "Ah . . . I seem to have hit upon something wood nymphs feel strongly about."

* * * *

Wickerdun entered the dining room and stopped. So far, he'd put off eating in here, unwilling to face the unpleasant memories this room carried. He'd dressed for dinner, his usual custom. Perhaps it was silly, but he felt more in control when formally attired. However, he didn't think it would help tonight. Thomas hovered nearby and Mrs. Littlepond peeked out from the service door. Unfortunately, someone had seen him talking aloud as he lay on the ground in the wood earlier, and had promptly reported his unusual behavior to Thomas. And Thomas, it would seem, had felt duty bound to spread the tale. He'd had servants looking at him all day, their expression one of expectation. Of what, he had no idea. Possibly that he break out in maniacal laughter while flinging off his clothes.

"You may serve, Thomas," Wickerdun said. "And yes, I feel fine."

Wickerdun stared at the other end of the table. Instead of picturing his mother, it was Megara's image he saw. He smiled. Yes, he could picture her seated thusly, perhaps with a plume in her hair. Megara wore plumes well. Added to her height. He chuckled. Why hadn't he considered her height before? She was tall for a woman, taller than most men, while faeries were short of stature. Or were they? He frowned.

"My lord? Is something wrong?"

"No, Thomas." He turned to face the older man. "I was wondering whether faeries were short or tall." Ha! Let him chew on that.

"Oh, they can be any size, my lord," Thomas replied. "Same as regular folk. Now, you got different clans, so to speak, different folk altogether, so some are always tall, some are hairier and such like."

Wickerdun blinked and then narrowed his eyes. "I was talking to wood nymphs today. What do you say to that?"

Thomas beamed. "Oh, wood nymphs! Well, that's all right then. We feared you were losing your traces, my lord." He turned to the service door. "Did you hear, Mrs. Littlepond? Our boy has found the wood nymphs." Thomas turned quickly. "Begging your pardon, my lord."

Were they having a jest at his expense? No, he didn't believe so. He pursed his lips. If they accepted what he said as truth . . .

"The woman I hope to marry introduced me to their songs."

Thomas's knees buckled, and Wickerdun shot from his chair. "Mrs. Littlepond!"

Mrs. Littlepond burst open the door and was at his side before the echo of his words died. "He'll be fine, my lord. Just the excitement about the new countess. Thomas has it in his head he can't leave service until he sees you wed to a proper lady and your heir safely born."

"Cannot leave?" Wickerdun shook his head. What an odd notion. Thomas looked white around his mouth, but was smiling up at him. "Sorry to disappoint you, Thomas, but she has not accepted me yet. My coming here was some sort of test. Of what I have no idea," he muttered. "Thomas, I insist you retire for the night."

* * * *

The breakfast room held no terror from the past. His father never ate in here that Wickerdun could recall. Still, Wickerdun saw Megara seated at the table rather than his mother. No plumes, but then Wickerdun had spent a restless night imagining what he'd do with a plume and Megara. He chewed his food with abandon. Would Megara enjoy bed-play? If she protested, he'd remind her she said she wanted to race, not trot. That brought a smile to his lips. By Jupiter, he'd teach that filly how to race! He chuckled and then choked. Had he referred to Megara as a *filly*? He leaned back in his chair, staring into space. That sounded like something his father would have said. Good God, was it starting in him?

He jumped up from the table and fled to the quiet of the wood. He needed time to think.

"You can understand my dilemma," Wickerdun said to the wood nymphs as he leaned his back against a tree. How freely he did that now, when just a short time ago he didn't even believe in them. "I would sooner end my existence than harm Megara. However, I feel my existence would lose all meaning if Megara was not by my side, was not my wife." He knocked the back of his head against the tree. "I sound pathetic." He concluded the excited chattering signaled agreement.

* * * *

Ardmoor leaned to rap on the coach window, but Megara's face was pressed against the glass. "We are here," he shouted. "About bloody time, too," he muttered as he urged his horse forward.

Megara exited the coach and looked up at Fairhills Hall. How beautiful! Her attention was drawn to the wood and she smiled. William was in the wood and talking to the wood nymphs! Oh, she wanted to kiss that man! Her aunt noisily descended and Megara turned to deal with her, then their baggage, and finally to the man who hobbled out to have a look at them. His hopes, his expression, brought a tear to her eye.

"Be you the woman our master wishes to wed?" he asked.

"He has got a bit of the blood in him," Aunt Susan said softly.

Megara smiled at the man, seeing a kindred spirit, her aunt's whispered words confirming what she'd seen.

"I hope I am." She smiled when the man laughed.

* * * *

A mere hour later after settling her aunt for a nap, Megara hurried down the stairs. She sensed Ardmoor's impatience before she heard the tapping of his peg. She was grateful to both Ardmoor and her aunt. Neither had wanted to come with her to Leicestershire, but they had.

"I am coming," she called.

About bloody time.

"I heard that," Megara said as she came to a halt before Ardmoor. "Your thoughts are as loud as spoken words, Trevor." She laughed at his arched brow. "Ardmoor."

"You need go to Wickerdun before the bl—silly wood nymphs chatter us up a cyclone. Do what you came to do so we can return to London. I shall remain at a discreet distance."

"You needn't bother, he is only—"

"I came as chaperone, Meg," Ardmoor said. "And yes, you need a chaperone. I can smell the man's lust."

Megara sniffed, but couldn't detect anything unusual. At his pained expression, she laughed. "Oh, you meant metaphorically speaking."

"No." He propelled her to the door, held open by Thomas. "I meant literally. Obviously, you cannot identify what I do, but Wickerdun is near the end of his tether, I fear. He knows he wants you, but has no clue as to why he is at such odds with himself."

Megara gave Ardmoor an admiring glance as they made their way toward William. "You can smell all of that? I am impressed."

Ardmoor grunted. "I am a male. I understand Wickerdun. The problem, dear Meg, is Wickerdun is caught in Cupid's man-trap, unable—"

"Man-trap? Do you not mean shot by Cupid's arrow?"

"No, man-trap. That is how love feels to a man. Trapped and unable to move no matter how you twist and turn, completely pole-axed by the pain of it all. Wondering why you cannot think clearly, make logical decisions. Then, lust enters into the mix. It is horrible. On top of that, Wickerdun is accepting his wild blood only now. For a true stick-in-the-mud like him, that must—"

"Yes," Megara broke in, "I realize all of that. It is the reason I felt compelled to come to him. And William is not a stick-in-the-mud, not anymore, not once he accepts his destiny to race with me. Now tell me more about man-traps and lust."

May God help Wickerdun.

"I heard that!"

* * * *

Wickerdun's eyes opened wide. Did he, or did he not just hear, *and understand,* the wood nymphs' song? Megara was here? At first a chorus of welcoming to Megara, they then sang about his loneliness coming to an end, which switched to an earthy song of praise for Megara and her soft-footed steps upon the ground. They spent so much time singing about her feet and soft-footedness, Wickerdun wasn't surprised he started tapping one foot in time to their song. They sang about the perfection of her firm body, the detail holding him enthralled. When they sang of the varied ways she and he might find delight in one another, Wickerdun imagined each scenario, promising himself the pleasure of introducing those delights to Megara. His gaze searched the path that would bring her to him. Still no sign of her, Wickerdun thumped his head. *Why was he waiting?* He would meet her. Of course! He ran.

"William!" Megara cried as she ran toward her love.

"Bloody hell!" Ardmoor bellowed. "Get back, Meg! The man is in full, bloody wood nymph-induced-lust! Wickerdun! Stand down!"

Megara froze. She'd never heard of wood nymph-induced-lust, but Ardmoor appeared to know about these things. William's face was flushed, and he was breathing hard. William pointed at her.

"She is mine, Ardmoor. You had your chance."

Her stomach fluttered at William's declaration. "Of course . . ." She stopped at Ardmoor's glare.

"As you say, Wickerdun, I had my chance. Alas, Lady Megara is unattached, although you say she is yours."

"She is mine," he said, his voice near a growl. Megara placed her hand over her rapidly beating heart. She smiled when Wickerdun's gaze raked possessively over her body. The thought crossed her mind he was picturing her without her clothes on. Her smile grew larger.

"Ah!" Ardmoor looked between the two. "Did I miss the announcement?"

Wickerdun looked at Ardmoor. "What?" He shook his head as if to clear it, then looked back at her. "What announcement?"

"Your betrothal," Ardmoor said.

Wickerdun took a step closer. "She will not say yes." He took another step. "But it occurs to me if—"

"Wickerdun!" Ardmoor snapped. "You are a gentleman, sir!"

William stopped and looked between her and Ardmoor. Megara stamped her foot when William pressed his hands to his head. He looked to be coming out of his lust.

* * * *

"I can climb the steps without assistance, Thomas. I am not injured, I tell you!" Wickerdun said. He still felt odd, as if every fiber of his body was on alert. And randy. Ready and randy, even now, especially when Megara was close.

"He will be fine," Ardmoor assured Thomas. "Bit of the old nymph -induced-lust." Ardmoor turned to Megara. "Poorly done, that."

Wickerdun's brows rose. Megara had caused that?

"I swear I had nothing to do with their song!" Megara raced up the steps and ran in front of him, her expression concerned. "You believe me, do you not, William?" she asked as she walked backwards. "Whatever happened to you, please know I did not incite them."

"I suppose they just happened to decide to work Wickerdun into a lather all by themselves?"

"How dare you imply I would do something so unethical!" Her gaze swung back to him. Wickerdun looked from her aqua eyes large and bright, to her trembling pink, moist lips. "I would never do that to someone, especially you, William."

Wickerdun grasped Ardmoor by the arm before he did something rash, like grab Megara and carry her away. "Could we possibly discuss this in a more private setting? Then you can explain what happened to me," he muttered.

Wickerdun didn't anticipate such a long wait. After they assembled in the drawing room, Ardmoor and Megara started in on one another. He stood by the hearth, waiting for Ardmoor and Megara to make peace. He told them he wouldn't listen to another word until they settled their differences. Their argument wasn't difficult to follow, except for the finer point of what it all meant. It had obviously struck a nerve with Ardmoor, and Megara was as insulted as if she'd been called a light-skirt. They finally made up, but not before Thomas entered with refreshments and forgot to leave. Wickerdun didn't have the heart to tell the old servant to go, and helped him to a seat near the door before the man dropped from excitement.

"Gladdened to see you have stopped throwing visual daggers at one another," he said as he sat near the two.

"I have to confess, my—what did you call it, Ardmoor? No, never mind. Let us say the unusual state I experienced out there." He grimaced. "Would it have affected me if I had not been able to understand them?"

All eyes turned upon him.

"You understood their song?" Megara asked. Her voice was near a whisper, but touched him like a caress. He nodded. "Oh, William!" she cried and jumped from her seat.

Ardmoor hauled her back. "Is not safe yet."

Wickerdun arched his brows in question. The question of why his inquiry evoked such a response in Megara paled beside his yearning for her. He turned to Ardmoor when the man cleared his throat.

"The fact you understood their song, and apparently liked what you heard, increased the suggestion. When they saw that, which they took as approval, they would have continued in a similar vein. Think of it as music to prepare a warrior before battle. It stimulated you."

Wickerdun rolled his eyes. An understatement if he ever heard one.

"When did you begin understanding the wood nymphs?" Megara asked.

"He understands wood nymphs?" Aunt Susan asked as she entered, looking at him in surprised approval. He and Ardmoor rose, although Wickerdun turned so his bulge wouldn't offend. She sat next to Megara.

"Today," he replied. "They informed me Lady Megara had arrived. That was the first time I understood them."

"You had been talking to them as well?" Megara said.

Wickerdun inclined his head. "I had no one else to talk to." Odd he no longer felt a fool for admitting he talked to wood nymphs.

Megara turned a smug expression toward Ardmoor. "See? He needed me. And, as you are undoubtedly aware, Ardmoor, wood nymphs delight in being noticed. Although he could not understand them, they understood every word he said to them." She turned to face him. "It would appear whatever you confided to them was the deciding factor in today's nymph-induced-lust."

"Mercy!" Aunt Susan cried and turned to look at her niece. "Are you—"

"I am fine, aunt," Megara replied. She turned back to him, her smile warm.

Wickerdun's arousal was near painful. He returned her smile, his body clamoring for more. He ignored her aunt's glare. "Are you saying they meant for me to . . .?" He stopped, unsure how to phrase what couldn't be said in front of ladies.

"Carry through to a natural conclusion," Ardmoor said. "Yes, that is exactly what they meant for you to do." He leaned close to whisper. "Later, I shall tell you the consequences of today's debacle."

Wickerdun wasn't reassured by the grim lines around Ardmoor's mouth. Had the same once happened to Ardmoor? As for the consequences, he believed he already knew; a constant arousal. Not necessarily a bad thing, but deuced awkward until he and Megara would marry. The thought of which brought images of them naked on a bed. He twisted in his seat, swallowing a moan. First things first. She had to agree to wed him.

"Are you in pain?" Megara asked.

Obviously, he hadn't stifled his moan. He gripped the chair seat to keep his hands off of her. "No pain." Pain didn't begin to describe the agony he felt. The aunt's snigger drew his attention.

"Well, Megara," her aunt said, "it looks as if you will be wedding very soon."

Megara looked to her aunt. "Why?"

"If you want to keep Wickerdun from suffering, you will marry post haste."

Her eyes were wide when she looked at him. "Oh, William, you are in pain!"

He shook his head, tearing his gaze from her. "Not pain." He jumped when Ardmoor slapped him on the back. It was difficult to keep his attention focused on something other than lying with Megara. He wanted to marry her, but didn't like the idea she might feel forced into accepting him. There had been a reason she hesitated, but for the life of him, he couldn't recall what it was.

"For the present," Ardmoor said as he rose, "I believe the ladies should remove themselves so Wickerdun and I can talk."

Megara shook her head. "Oh, but I came here to—"

"Come along, Megara," her aunt said, "and I shall explain the ways of things."

Wickerdun scowled at the aunt's snigger. He truly hoped she wouldn't live with them.

* * * *

"You have evaded and danced around my questions, Ardmoor. Will I ever be normal? By Jupiter, a man cannot live like this without a serious hurt done to him!"

He sat sprawled in a chair while Ardmoor stood by a window, looking out.

"You are bloody well done for, Wickerdun." Ardmoor turned. "Get used to your state until you and Megara wed. It should lessen after that, but you shall never be normal again. You can thank your wild blood for this bleeding *gift*."

Lessen. It would lessen. Wickerdun nodded. "When will I be able to think clearly again?"

Ardmoor cracked a smile. "Your faculties will return, slowly. Which brings me to the point of marriage." Ardmoor sat near. "I know you want to be with Megara. I know it is constantly running through your mind. But are you able to separate your physical want and overwhelming desire for her from your thinking part? The question of marriage. Can you think clearly long enough to decide if that is what you want?"

"Of course I want Megara. To marry her." Wickerdun looked to the door. He should be talking to Megara, not Ardmoor. If Megara agreed, they could wed soon. He'd get a special license.

"Concentrate, Wickerdun! You are still feeling the effects of the nymph-induced-lust, one of which is the desire to be with Megara. Think, man! You came here to do something. Did you succeed?"

Wickerdun shut his eyes. Try as he might, he couldn't pull his thoughts together long enough to remember. The face of his mother came suddenly to mind. The image of her bending over him, covering him. Protecting him. He was perhaps five years old. Her whispering in his ear, telling him to pretend he didn't have any gifts, because that would keep him safe from his father. She told him he'd remember his gifts one day, and when he did, for him to use them wisely.

Wickerdun opened his eyes. "Bloody hell."

"What is it, Wickerdun? You look—"

"I am not like my father." Wickerdun turned to Ardmoor, noting the concern in the man's eyes. *No, he could . . . smell? Smell Ardmoor's concern.* He grinned. What other talents might he have?

"No, you bloody well are not. You never were," Ardmoor agreed. "How do you feel?"

Wickerdun took a deep breath. He felt wonderful! His head was clear, his body hummed with joy in being alive. His arousal was strong, but under control. How extraordinary! He'd not have thought it possible to have such control over his willy. He looked at Ardmoor and laughed. "I feel magnificent!"

* * * *

Megara looked up when Ardmoor entered the morning room alone. "Where is William? Is he—"

"Wickerdun is magnificent. Those are his words, not mine. He looks as though he has come to terms with whatever devil was biting at his heels."

Just what she wanted to hear! Happiness filled her, but she wanted to know more details. "Where is he?"

"Went for a long ride."

He went for a ride? "What? Does he not want to see me?"

Ardmoor arched his brow at her. "After his ride, I suggested he swim. For the rest of the day."

Megara rose. Really!   "Ardmoor, the water will be freezing! All I want to do is talk to him. If you recall, that was my purpose in coming here."

"If you care for Wickerdun, you will leave him alone today."

"I agree," Aunt Susan said. "The wedding simply cannot be held sooner than six months, twelve would be best, what with—"

Megara swallowed her anger and sat. "William and I shall choose the date for our wedding. *If,"*—she glared at both Ardmoor and her aunt—"he and I ever have an opportunity to be alone so he can ask me to marry him."

"You've decided?" Ardmoor asked.

Megara nodded. "Mrs. Littlepond and Thomas were a font of information. Based on what they told me, what I knew, and William's acceptance of his blood, I decided to accept his offer. *If* we can ever be alone long enough—"

"Did you get a look at the housekeeper?" Aunt Susan asked Ardmoor.

"Short, squat, flat nose and wide smile? Looks like a frog?"

Her aunt nodded. "*Littlepond*." She tapped her finger to her nose. "I would wager a small fortune her roots come from the water."

Megara smiled. Wonder what William would say to that.

* * * *

It wasn't a plume, but it would do. Wickerdun brushed the feather across Megara's lips. She turned her head slightly. He continued to graze the feather across her face, down her neck, and then across the night rail over her breasts. When she didn't wake, he kissed her softly on her lips.

Megara woke to find the object of her fancy kissing her— as he had been doing in her dream. His stare, so close, ignited flames to dance from her woman's core to her heart. She followed when he pulled away.

"Do not tempt me," he whispered. "I am barely hanging on here. Ardmoor threatened to unman me if I forced myself on you before our wedding. But I had to see you."

His words sent shivers of anticipation up her spine. "I am glad you came to me." The heated look in his eyes drew her to his lips. Once again, he pulled away.

"We need to talk, Megara," he whispered, alternately sucking and kissing her fingers. "I want to marry you, you know that. But I do not want you to feel forced to accept me because of my condition. A condition only you can help. Will you marry me, Megara? I am ready to race with you. Look forward to racing with you. Running and racing."

Megara moaned each time his tongue threaded between her fingers. If she hadn't already made up her mind to say yes, and she could think clearly, she might have been annoyed with his use of lust as a deciding factor. As it was, she knew he couldn't help himself. "Yes, William, I will marry you. When?" She sat up when he moved toward the window. What was he doing? He was leaving? "Are you not going to kiss me?"

"Shhh! If I kiss you I would not stop. Best wait until tomorrow."

He wanted to wait until tomorrow? Did he have one leg out her window? "Are you going out the window?"

"Shhh! That is the way I came. I have discovered I have extraordinary climbing abilities. Among other things."

She caught a bit of his thought. Rather intriguing. "Like what?"

"Shhh! We will talk tomorrow."

"But . . ." He disappeared into the night. Megara beat the bed with her fists.

* * * *

"It is settled then? September?" Wickerdun asked, rubbing his hands together. "Megara? You agree to a September wedding?"

She turned and smiled at Wickerdun. "I agree to a September wedding." Her heart ached whenever she looked at Wickerdun's blackened eyes.

Her gaze narrowed on Ardmoor. "Provided my husband-to-be is hale and hearty." *I will get you for that!*

Ardmoor bowed to her and smirked. "I heard that."

"However, I do not agree we need to be separated until then," she said. "I want to enjoy the rest of the Season with William. It will look odd if his future countess is nowhere to be seen. It might cause talk and speculation."

"Pish posh, who cares what people think?" Aunt Susan exclaimed. "That is what you always said, is it not?"

Megara glared at her aunt. "This is different. William has a seat in parliament. His reputation and influence could be ruined by gossip and speculation."

"*And* blue unicorns," Ardmoor added to her aunt. "She is right, Wickerdun. You cannot announce your betrothal and have her vanish. Are you up . . . er, can you handle the stress of her being near? For five months?"

Megara rolled her gaze to the ceiling. Why had she involved Ardmoor and her aunt?

Wickerdun smiled as he took in the scene. There was warmth here, and deep caring despite the irritation currently held by all. Ardmoor protective of Megara, yet also concerned about his political future. Aunt Susan, master tactician at saying just the right thing to get Megara to agree to what she wanted. And Megara, who just wanted to be with him. All of them concerned with his reputation, something that had mattered a great deal to him only a week ago. For the first time in decades, he felt he belonged, that he was part of a family that looked out for one another, who cared.

Five months? God, yes!

Chapter Four
Song of the Wood Nymphs

"The sound is deafening," Megara said as she looked out the window to the wood. "I doubt any of the family will be able to sleep." She turned and smiled at her husband of eight hours. "I have never heard them so happy. What is that chuckle for? And why do you look so pleased with yourself?"

"After five months of waiting, you have to ask?"

Megara tilted her head. "There is more to it than that."

Wickerdun pulled her into his arms, and kissed the top of her head. "You know me well, Meg. Yes, there is more. A surprise, one I hope you will like. Now that the time is upon me though, I am not sure. I had not considered our guests." He didn't let her pull away. "But you will not hear my gift until we are in bed."

"In bed?"

He chuckled at the strange notions floating out of her head. "I wrote a poem for you, my dearest Meg. The wood nymphs said they would sing it for us."

"But only when we are in bed?"

"It is a bed song," he whispered, kissing her ear. "Of course, it is primarily a love song. I tried to write about the love I have for you, the joy of knowing we will be together forever, my happiness every time I see you. My efforts seemed feeble, so the wood nymphs said they would sing it as a bed song. My hope is when you hear their song you will understand how much I love you."

Her sigh was all he needed to hear. He picked her up and carried her to his bed.

* * * *

"Sleep well?"

Ardmoor arched his brow at Maddy, then turned his gaze to Spode. "My sister suffers the delusion of being a wit. Between the bloody singing all night, the bloody laughter coming from all the married couples, more bloody singing, no, I did not sleep well!" He rose and marched from the room.

Maddy and Spode looked at one another in surprise. "I have not seen Ardmoor like that since . . . never," Maddy said. "What do you think . . .?"

"He needs a woman," Spode declared.

"I do not need a woman," Ardmoor said from the doorway. "Came back to apologize." He pointed his finger at his sister and brother-in-law. "Do not start meddling in my life."

Only And Always You

Chapter One
Avoiding the Obvious

Harry gazed around the ballroom, seeking his hosts, the Earl and Countess of Spode. Time to extend his appreciation for their invitation and bid his farewell. He'd reached his limit for socializing. At least Spode's ballroom was fitted with a wall of doors that opened to the garden. A man could escape through those doors from time to time to suck in fresh air. One had to be careful though, lest some young thing trailed after one with the ignoble intention of becoming his viscountess by arranging to be caught in a compromising position. Harry Wilkerson, Viscount Seton, was careful. He'd avoided all traps set for him by marriage-minded misses and their formidable mothers for sixteen years. At age thirty-four, he wasn't about to be caught. Not now, when the last of his sisters was to be launched, and hopefully soon married. Then he could retire from society.

His gaze fell on a woman across the room and his heart skipped a beat, but she disappeared before he could determine if . . . No, Claire was in India. Although people did return home from there. What if it was Claire? He had nothing to say to her.

Harry studied the women on the far side of the room. Claire's red hair was distinctive, but he saw no red headed woman. Just as well. Although it might be amusing to hear her excuses and justifications. Yes, and then he'd grant her an icy smile before turning and walking away. That would show her how little—

"Harry! Bloody Viscount Seton!"

Harry turned. "Ardmoor." He inclined his head toward Ardmoor's peg leg. "Nice bow."

Ardmoor picked up his leg to look. "Bloody hell! Forgot my niece decorated it for me."

Harry frowned. "Yes, sisters and nieces do the strangest things. Never understood them."

"Ha! You bloody well never will. Hear your youngest sister gets launched next week."

Harry nodded. "Finally. Been making the rounds to ensure Felicity's ball will be well attended. Be relieved when it's over and I can retire to Seton Hall. Hate these events."

"Your mother . . . ?"

Harry sighed and shifted on his feet. "Claims she's too weak to go out. She's not. It's her way to get me out in society where she hopes I'll find someone, wed and produce an heir." He stiffened when he saw Claire. It *was* her! What the devil was she doing in London? Had she and her little weasel of a husband returned from India?

"Shall I introduce you?"

Harry whipped his head around. "Introduce me?"

"To Lady Claire. She was the one you were bloody well gawking at, was she not?"

"By Jupiter, no!" Harry cleared his throat. "That is, I'm well acquainted with Claire. Her. Lady Claire. Not that well acquainted!" he snapped upon sight of Ardmoor's raised brows. "She married my mother's godson and they went to India. Ten years ago."

"She's just returned," Ardmoor said. "My sister Maddie had her to dinner before tonight's ball. Lovely woman."

"I wasn't aware the countess and Lady Claire were acquainted."

"When Maddie made her debut, she said Claire was kind to her, since they both have red hair. They've corresponded for years, apparently. Maddie urged her to return when she learned she was a widow."

Harry looked back at Claire. "She's a widow?" *No doubt on the prowl for another title.* "How unfortunate."

Ardmoor snorted. "It bloody well isn't. The man was infamous. His luck ran out with his last duel. He left behind a mountain of debts and notes, but many relieved husbands."

"It surprises me to hear Lady Claire would confess such things at the dinner table." *Doubtless she counted on gaining everyone's sympathy. Little does she realize . . .*

"Ha! To listen to her, her days in India were bloody idyllic. No, talk's been trickling back from India for years about Stauton-West. If you ever conversed with anyone when you went to your clubs, you'd have known this."

Harry pursed his lips. "The old adage, 'Marry in haste, repent in leisure', appears to apply in her case."

"Wed Stauton-West suddenly, did she?"

"Three weeks by special license."

"Someone was in a hurry, weren't they?"

Chapter Two
Ice Water Seton

"Really, Claire! You can't hide behind the potted plants all evening!"

Claire smoothed her gown. "I'm not hiding, Maddie. I found a spot with a breeze and I'm claiming it for my own. Why should I hide?"

"To avoid Viscount Seton? Ardmoor said he saw you scurry away when Seton was announced. And watched as you fled from plant to plant to avoid coming face to face with the man."

Claire raised her chin. "I have no wish to see him. In truth, he's the last man, the *only* man I have no wish to see or to speak to." Claire turned from Maddie's knowing eyes. "Ever."

"He never wed, you know."

Claire lifted a shoulder. "Duty to family came first ten years ago, so I expect it still does."

"He never misses a session of parliament."

"Laudable."

"I hear his mother is frantic for him to wed and produce an heir."

Lord, is that battle-axe still alive? "I'm sure there are more than enough women willing to oblige her." *Until they meet his mother. They'd have to be desperate to endure that dragon.*

"Indeed there are. But Seton rarely shows himself during the season. When he does he never smiles, let alone indicate a preference for any one woman. You can set your watch to the two hours he allows himself before correctly taking his leave." Maddy leaned forward and laughed. "He's known as Ice Water Seton amongst the ton."

Claire frowned. He'd certainly changed from the laughing, amiable young man who broke her heart.

* * * *

"Zounds, Maddie!" Spode said. "Are you and your brother plotting to bring Seton and Lady Claire together?"

Ardmoor watched his sister blush before she raised her chin and faced her husband. "We are. It was obvious to us they still have feelings for one another."

"Because she hid herself from his view and he departed before he might have to face her?" Spode asked.

"You will cease such facetiousness at once, *if you please!*"

Ardmoor saw Spode's smile widen as the man rocked on his heels. "Actually, my love, if you and Ardmoor succeed with this latest endeavor, I think it would be the saving of Seton. He acts like a man twice his age. Lady Claire might have more years to her than a man seeking a wife would like, but she would rescue him from himself. What can I do to help your efforts?"

"Oh, Robert!" Ardmoor snorted when Maddie launched herself into her husband's waiting arms.

* * * *

"Harry! The Countess of Spode has invited me to tea this afternoon!"

Harry looked up from his plate and swallowed. His sister sounded inordinately pleased. "No doubt because I attended their ball last evening." The image of Claire intruded and the movement of fork to mouth halted. Her image had intruded into his thoughts all bloody night long. He pushed thoughts of Claire from his mind. The *widow* Claire.

His sister gave a tiny squeal and smiled whilst waving her letter. "She says you and I are invited to join them in a picnic of a small, select group of friends!"

Harry grunted and faced his breakfast plate. "I'm sure you will enjoy yourself."

"You're not going?"

"Too busy."

"You don't even know when . . ."

Harry put down his fork and arched his brow. "I do not attend picnics. They're silly. A waste of time." His arched brow fell when his sister's eyes fill with tears. "What? I didn't say you couldn't attend, only that *I'm* not attending."

"You *are* Ice Water Seton!"

Chapter Three
A Young Girl's Innocent Candor and Untarnished Dreams

"A pleasure to meet you, Lady Claire," Lady Felicity said. "I'm so very interested in India. I hear so many stories, and I can't credit they're all true, but I do so hope they are! If I were a man, I'd travel to India. Actually, I'd travel all over the world if I were a man, and not just India. Visiting only one country seems too restrictive, don't you agree?"

Claire kept her smile in place and nodded at Lady Felicity, before turning to give Maddie a surreptitious glare. Why had Maddie invited Harry's sister to their *private* tea?

Maddie returned her glare with a sunny smile.

"Since I am not a man, I shall," Lady Felicity continued, "before I marry, make sure my future husband is inclined to travel and having adventures. That way . . ."

Claire covered her mouth. Apparently her snort was louder than intended. "Pardon me."

Lady Felicity gave her a large, conspiratorial smile and continued talking.

Claire listened, charmed by the young girl's innocent candor and untarnished dreams and desires. Her hair was blonde, lighter than her brother's. They both had the same clear blue eyes. Claire wondered if she and Harry had married and had children, would they have had her red hair and brown eyes? Or would they favor Harry? Possibly a mix of the two?

"Actually," Maddie said to Felicity, "wagers were made that Lady Claire and Seton would wed before the season was over."

Claire started. When had the conversation changed? Lady Felicity was looking at her in wonderment.

"Oh, why didn't you marry him!" Felicity cried. "I remember when he used to laugh and joke and be . . . well, be a rather wonderful brother, warm and good-natured. Now he counts the hours until he can return to Seton Hall. He sees no one, does nothing. He is Ice Water Seton!" Felicity turned to Maddie. "Do you know what he said to me when I told him about the picnic invitation?"

He sees no one, does nothing. What made Harry change? Has he found duty too exacting a love? Well, that had been his choice when he rejected her. Still, Claire wasn't comfortable in hearing about Harry's slow but steady decline into curmudgeon-hood.

"So he'll attend?" Maddie asked.

Felicity nodded. "He looked so confused by my tears, and my reference to his being Ice Water Seton completely flummoxed him. He stared at me briefly, as if I were some strange new plant he'd stumbled upon and then assured me he would attend." Felicity turned to Claire. "I know this is an improper question, but I must know. May I ask why you and my brother never wed? Was your late husband the better man?"

Claire flicked a look at Maddie before she spoke. "Your brother told me his duty to family and title precluded marriage between us. Although I was born a member of the gentry, my birth was deemed too low to form a connection with your family. I was informed I was unsuitable because of my Irish grandparents. "

"Oh."

Claire rose. "I must be off. It was good to meet you Lady Felicity, and I wish you well this season. A word of warning, if I may. Don't rush into a betrothal or allow yourself to be pushed to a hasty decision. Wait at least six months to fully know your future husband. I know this goes against all we're told, but men can be devious, presenting only their good façade whilst hiding their true natures. I'm sure he will, but have your brother carefully check their finances. Some men seek only the financial rewards marriage can bring, pretending affection that isn't present at all. Your brother will understand."

Chapter Four
The Image of Claire Intrudes

Harry looked up when his sister presented herself before his desk, her hands on her hips. "The tea didn't go well?"

"*How could you!*"

He sighed. It appeared they were now going to play the guessing game that females loved to win. He really would be relieved when the last of his sisters was out of the house. "How could I do what?"

"Tell Lady Claire her family wasn't good enough for you!"

Harry shot up, sending his papers flying across his desk. "Where did you see that woman?"

"At the—"

"She told you I said she wasn't good enough?" He laughed shortly. "Just like her to twist my words. I told her duty to family was of paramount importance, and I didn't expect to wed anytime soon. I told her she should put herself forward if she hoped to contract a suitable marriage." He glared at his sister. "Close your mouth."

"You told her—"

"Before you chastise me further, may I ask if she told you she wed within three weeks of our conversation?" Harry nodded at her shocked expression. "That tells you how much affection she held for me. Mother was right, Claire was only interested in my title. Little did Claire know, but I was prepared to offer for her. Mother urged me to wait and see if Claire's affection would hold true. It didn't." Harry arched a brow. "The subject is closed."

Claire drew her brows together. "She told me to wait for at least six months before I agreed to a betrothal."

Harry snorted. "'Marry in haste, repent at leisure'."

"She also said to make sure you carefully check my future husband's finances, because some men marry for financial reward rather than affection. She said you would know all about that."

Harry leaned across his desk until Felicity stepped back. "On that she is correct. I know exactly how to protect you, just as I have all your other sisters. The subject, as I said before, is closed."

Felicity looked down. "I think it sad she was married for her dowry. I like her. Even if she did marry the first man to ask her because you told her she wasn't good enough."

Harry walked around his desk and grasped his sister by her arm, escorting her to the door. "She *had* no dowry to speak of, so she's lying about that. Like her if you choose, just don't mention her to me. And I *never* said she wasn't good enough." He closed the door behind her.

"Why did you object to her grandparents?"

Harry flung open the door. "What grandparents?"

"Her Irish grandparents."

Harry slammed and locked the door.

* * * *

Ardmoor and Spode alighted from the carriage, continuing their conversation.

"Maddie reminded me Seton's mother didn't like the idea of Lady Claire becoming Seton's wife all those years ago. Could possibly kick up a fuss this time around," Spode said.

"Ah," Ardmoor said. "If Seton didn't pay Stauton-West's debts, do you suppose it was his mother? Stauton-West was the mother's godson, according to Seton."

"A bribe? She'll pay his debts if he marries the girl and keeps her away from her son?"

"Exactly. Except I don't understand why Lady Claire accepted Stauton-West's suit so bloody quick if she was supposed to be in love with Seton."

"Maddie explained it to me."

After stating their wish to see Seton, Spode hurriedly explained.

"Good sign he agreed to see us," Spode told Ardmoor as they were shown to Seton's study. "He's never home to anyone. The luck of our Wild blood is with us."

Ardmoor grunted. "Why doesn't he visit his bloody clubs like other men? Damned preposterous to pretend we've run into him in his own home."

* * * *

Harry sat at his desk, neatening his papers, the image of Claire intruding. Why return into his life now? Couldn't she have waited another month or so until Felicity was married off? Then he'd be away at Seton Hall, far from her distracting presence. He sat back. Wait six months before agreeing to wed? If people waited that long to know one another, no one would ever agree to wed anyone.

Silly notion.

Had she really wed the first man to ask because he spurned her? Or was his mother correct that Claire had only been interested in a title? And why, in God's name, had she accepted Stauton-West? It was a slap in his face when he heard she wed the knave. A wastrel, rake, and gamester. What had her father been about to grant his permission? Ah, but her parents had been called out of the country and she'd been staying with her aunt and uncle.

Harry drummed his fingers on his desk. Claire's dowry had been less than modest. Stauton-West was always in debt. Yet they had sailed to India. Had Stauton-West left his debts behind? Is that why they departed so quickly?

He decided his preoccupation with Claire was the reason he unaccountably agreed to see his visitors.

Chapter Five
It was the Dragon

Harry sat in his box at the theater and stared across the distance into Spode's box. Claire was amongst the Spode's and their friends. Appeared to be having a fine time, what with everyone laughing. Harry ignored Felicity's excited chatter beside him. He wished she would keep quiet, but allowed as she didn't require answers to her questions, he'd let her ramble.

Claire thought he paid Stauton-West to marry her? What nonsense. She'd hidden behind potted plants to avoid him? How ridiculous. Just like a woman to hide and avoid the issue. Why hadn't she accused him outright? It really was utter nonsense.

What could possibly be so amusing that had everyone in Spode's box laughing?

At intermission, Harry turned to his sister and asked if she would care to join him in visiting. "Close your mouth," he snapped.

* * * *

Claire saw Maddie nudge her husband the same time silence descended in their box. It lasted but a moment until everyone rushed to speak. During intermission, many had stopped by to visit with the Spode's, their guests, and renew their acquaintance with her. So whoever made an appearance, and Claire was turning to see who they might be, it must be short of astounding to cause such a reaction. Bits of conversation drifted to her, and her stomach clenched whilst heat and cold raced up and down her torso.

It couldn't be! Maddie and Spode swore Harry never attended the theater. But there he was, standing in the doorway, looking at her. Cold air swirled up her nose and she was struck by the sudden fear she might cast up her accounts. Still, she couldn't help but note how well Harry looked. Ten years older, but as handsome as ever. Voices came to her from a distance, which was odd. Then Harry charged toward her. What was he about, making a scene? This would be the grand topic around the breakfast tables in London tomorrow morning.

"Let me get her out to the corridor!" she heard him say. "Take your hands off her!" Claire wondered who he was speaking to, and why was his face so red? "Come with me, Lady Claire," he said. "You need fresher air."

Claire agreed. Her knees were wobbly and her head couldn't decide whether to throb or spin. "The dragon won't like this," she said, the comforting sensation of his one arm around her waist forcing her eyes closed. She gripped his other arm to keep from falling.

"Dragons?"

She opened her eyes upon hearing her name called, and felt the rush of cooler air on her face. She blinked in the near darkness. "Where am I?"

"Someone's carriage," Harry replied, chaffing her hands. "How do you feel?"

"What?" She pulled her hands from his. She could see the vague outline of his form but not his face. "Who's carriage?"

"I don't know. Wickerdun's or his brother. They'd just arrived when I carried you out."

"Carried . . ." Claire shoved Harry back and leaned toward the open door. She saw Spode, the earl of Wickerdun and his brother standing outside. She looked back at Harry. "Why did you carry me out here?"

"You fainted," he replied, sounding rather put out.

"I never faint," she snapped.

"You said something about dragons, and then you fainted."

Claire sat back and rubbed her temples. "I never faint." She looked in his direction when she heard him sigh. "I'm fine now." She gathered up her skirt and moved to the door.

"We need to talk before returning."

She paused and looked at Harry. She wished she could see his expression. "I don't think we have anything to talk about."

"We do," he said as he reached over and closed the door.

Before her words of outrage were uttered, the door was opened. Spode waggled his finger at Harry. "Close the door and you'll ruin Lady Claire's reputation."

"Then step away so we can speak privately," Harry snapped.

"There's nothing to talk about," Claire said. "Will you help me descend, Lord Spode?" She pinched her lips together when Spode looked toward Harry and said, "We'll give you three minutes."

Claire turned to glare at Harry, but with the darkness, she knew her glare went unnoticed. "What is it you wish to talk about?"

"What the devil do you mean by telling people I paid Stauton-West to marry you?"

"Didn't you?"

She heard the sound of, she thought, fist hitting door. "No! How could you believe such a thing of me?"

"Because Phillip told me he was paid handsomely to woo me, wed me, and take me out of the country."

"And you believed him?"

Claire cast her gaze to the carriage roof. "Yes. Why should I doubt him?"

"Because the man always lied! He didn't know how to tell the truth! He was a thief, a rake, a gamester. The man was no good!"

"Yes, I know."

Another fist-hitting-door sound. "Then why did you marry him?"

"Well *obviously* I didn't know all that before I married him. As you say, he was a liar, a very good liar. He persuaded me I was the love of his life. Said I was the most beautiful, wonderful girl he ever met, and never knew such happiness as he felt when in my presence, ad nauseam."

"And you believed him?"

Claire quelled the urge to strike her fist against Harry. "As I said, he was persuasive. As soon as we sailed, he reverted to his true character. I was stuck in bed with the Mal de Mere, and I admit, not feeling kindly toward anyone, especially Phillip, after learning his *surprise* marriage gift was a voyage to India. Phillip said he understood why you would pay to have me away from you."

"I didn't, I swear to you. Although I may be many things, I don't believe I'm capable of behaving that despicably."

She'd never wanted to believe Harry had paid Phillip to marry her. It gave her a small measure of pleasure to know he hadn't. Which meant if it wasn't Harry, then it was his mother. The dragon. "I believe you. Now may we return before we cause another scene?"

* * * *

Harry arrived at the park before dawn, his horse ready to run. He scanned the area looking for Claire. He'd been told she still rode early in the morning. Although Harry rode daily, he was a solitary rider. Never this area where he would meet others and have to talk.

"Where the devil is she?" he muttered. Up half the night thinking about her. Remembering how she felt in his arms, the floral scent she still favored . . . whatever it was, he never remembered whether it was rose or lilac. Lavender? A trace of which lingered on his coat. With the silent acknowledgement he'd lost his mind, Harry had held his coat to his nose whilst trying to sleep, inhaling the last whiffs of the flowery smell. Of Claire.

Whilst sniffing, he decided it prudent to make sure she believed he hadn't paid the little weasel to marry her. Then, too, it would be wise to make sure she hadn't suffered any ill effects from her faint. Did she faint often? She said not, but had she contracted some disease whilst in India? Damn Stauton-West for exposing her to an unhealthy climate! Claire had red hair and the fair complexion to match. Her skin burned quickly in the sun, and as he recalled, too much heat made her ill. That's why she liked the north. Loved Northumberland and its coast, Harry had been thrilled to hear, since his primary home was on the Northumberland coast. She enjoyed the country, just as he did. One of the many things they had in common. To be honest, he and Claire had shared many interests, held similar views on most things, and had always laughed at the same thing.

"By Jupiter!" he said aloud. Spode told him yesterday, to his intense displeasure, that he, Harry, hadn't laughed in years. Harry quickly disabused him of such a nonsensical opinion. Spode also said he was turning into an old man. Harry hadn't shown him the door, they were old friends after all, but Harry let it be known he didn't appreciate such wayward levity at his expense.

Felicity had called him Ice Water Seton.

Spode and Ardmoor mentioned that as well.

"By Jupiter!" he repeated. "I *am* turning into an old man."

Chapter Six
Love's Laughter

Claire turned her horse around to watch Harry ride away. Out of her life. Her gaze fell appreciatively on his broad back, admiringly on his seat, and approvingly on his muscular legs. The man was uncommonly handsome. She didn't believe Harry knew how handsome he was. Harry would never use his handsome looks to lure a woman to him. She sighed. He probably knew how attractive his smile was though, because he kept flashing his heart-skipping smile at her whilst all were gathered. His wit had surprised some in her group, judging from remarks made when he rode away. Spode said that was how Harry used to be. That was how Claire remembered him.

Why had he come? He'd asked if she was recovered from her indisposition of last evening. When she replied she was in the pink of health, he stared at her for a moment before giving her a smile and saying he was delighted by such good news. He then turned his charm on the rest of the riders. Whenever he turned to her to speak, Claire had turned away. He ceased trying to converse with her.

Why had he come? It would be so easy to open her heart to him again. And so very foolish.

* * * *

Harry bounded up the steps upon his return from his clubs. Four hours before the Hobbs's recital. Spode said Claire would be attending. He stopped before Johnson, wondering why the butler was looking at him so strangely. "Ah! I was whistling, wasn't I?"

"Yes, my lord."

Harry cocked his head. "I haven't whistled in a donkey's age, have I, Johnson?"

"No, my lord."

Harry whistled a short tune, and then laughed. "I'd forgotten how good it feels to whistle."

"Yes, my lord."

"*Harry?* Is that you, Harry? I told Johnson I wanted to see you immediately upon your arrival!"

Harry looked up to see his mother at the top of the stairs. He sighed.

"My lord, your mother . . ."

"I heard, Johnson. I heard."

* * * *

". . . and after that, Lady Forbes said she heard talk you and that woman were alone in the carriage for most of the night! Then you were seen riding with her this morning. I won't have it, Harry! That woman is out to get you, just like..."

"Mother, Lady Claire is not out to get me. As usual, your friends have the facts all wrong."

"But everyone, absolutely everyone, is talking about the interest you're showing in that woman."

Harry smiled. "I advise you to become inured of the talk, Mother, for I intend to pay particular attention to Lady Claire."

"She's out for your title! Money!"

Harry threw back his head and laughed. "She turned down an offer of marriage to an Italian count after she was widowed. As for money, when she arrived in London she learned she'd inherited a substantial amount from a grandparent."

"Her *Irish* grandparent."

Harry clenched his jaw. "I don't see that it matters whether the grandparent was Irish or English. No, Mother, she is not out for my title or money."

"Pretty lies she tells. And you are foolish to believe her, Harry!"

"No, Mother, my information came from visiting my clubs and talking to people. In truth, she behaves as if she abhors my very sight."

"An act. She's out to get you!"

Harry smiled as he thought of this morning. He'd stopped and turned to look, to catch another glimpse of Claire. She'd been staring after him. Caught in the act, she'd turned and galloped in the other direction, to catch up with her companions. After pretending a disinterest in him, Claire had been staring after him! "No, mother, she's not out to get me. I'm out to get her."

* * * *

Claire studied the programme and smiled when she saw Lady Emily, the earl of Spode's sister, was scheduled to play. Oooh, she was going to play a selection from Beethoven's Piano Sonata #14! She wished it was the entire—

The heat of his body hit her the instant his scent reached her nose. Claire turned to face Harry and called herself all kinds of fool when her stomach quivered at the sight of his smile.

"Good evening, Lady Claire."

It was difficult not to return his smile, but she succeeded. "You're sitting in my cousin's chair."

"Your cousin was happy to relinquish her chair to me. See, she's smiling. I think she likes me."

Claire looked where Harry pointed and saw Ellen smiling widely. No doubt her cousin thought she'd done Claire a good turn. She'd have to have a talk with Ellen.

"I like your feather," Harry drawled.

Claire pinched her lips together, but it was no use. His expression made her laugh out loud.

"Ah, I made you laugh. Do you recall how we used to try to get the other to laugh first?"

Claire nodded, still smiling. "Want to wear my feather?"

"It might clash with my clothes."

"No, feathers work well with black. We could stick it down your cravat, behind your head." When he shook his head she tapped him with her rolled up programme. "Imagine how regal you'd look each time you turned or inclined your head. A big, fluffy feather to accompany your every nod and command. You'd be known as Viscount Fluffy-Head."

His bark of laughter drew all eyes to them. She and Harry leaned forward toward one another and laughed. Claire laughed until she had to wipe her eyes, and looked at Harry. His expression drained the levity from her.

"Claire, can we . . .?"

"Ah, the music is about to begin," she said and whipped out her fan, keeping her eyes to the front.

* * * *

Harry didn't attend to the music. He was happy. Claire was back in his life and . . . When had he realized he still loved her? He thought back over the last two days, and decided it didn't matter. He loved her. If he wasn't mistaken, and he didn't think he was, she still felt something for him. Hopefully it was love. She was skittish around him, but he had rejected her all those years ago; he could appreciate her reluctance to trust. He understood, once Spode explained what his wife explained to him, that Claire had been so hurt by his rejection, her sense of worth nil, she accepted the first man to look upon her with approval. Having four sisters who cried when one looked at them 'funny,' Harry was acquainted with the female need for approval.

It was just a matter of time before he convinced her he cared for her and wanted her as his wife.

* * * *

Why was he displaying such attention? She couldn't credit . . . no, couldn't *allow* herself to believe his singular interest pointed toward marriage. Claire had forgotten his presence briefly, whilst Lady Emily played the pianoforte, but now the music was over. The time had come for her to face Harry and tell him she didn't want his consideration.

"Shall we have some refreshment?" he asked.

Claire nodded. This was going to be difficult. She'd never noticed how the sound of his voice flowed over her body like a caress. Had it always done? He handed her a glass of lemonade.

"May I escort you to the Spode picnic?"

Claire studied her glass. "I'm attending with my cousin."

"I shall escort you both. She likes me, remember?"

Claire smiled. He always made her smile. Well, not always. "I don't believe it wise for you to continue paying attention to me." She looked up when he didn't reply. He wore a slight frown.

"If you tell me you have absolutely no feeling for me, that you loath the very sight of me, I shall oblige you and never trouble you again."

The blasted man! "I . . ."

"But you must look me in the eye and tell me you loath me. Can you do that, Claire?"

Claire shook her head. "It isn't about how I feel. It's about—"

"Oh, but it is all about how you feel," he said. "This isn't an idle flirtation, Claire. I'm pursuing you. I want to marry you, if you'll have me. Something I should have done ten years ago."

Claire wrapped his words carefully around her heart. She would treasure them always. She shook her head and stepped back, before she did something impulsive, like accept his proposal. "Your mother dislikes me." She raised her chin when he rolled his eyes toward the ceiling. "You make it seem trivial, and it's not! Your mother would make our lives miserable if we wed. Such animosity can wreak havoc in a marriage. I won't have it. If I ever marry again, I intend to be as happy and content as possible."

"Mother will come around. I'll talk to her."

"No, Harry, she won't come around. To force the issue will only alienate everyone involved."

"Has she ever said anything to you?"

Claire forced a smile and sipped her lemonade before she spoke. If she told him the truth he might do something rash, and she didn't want to cause a division in his family. "Some things need not be said aloud."

"I refuse to believe this can't be resolved. By Jupiter, I do this in committees all the time! So, may I escort you and your cousin to the picnic?"

* * * *

Claire wasn't surprised when Lady Seton was announced the next day. Her aunt and cousin received the news with twitters and nervous smoothing of hair, cap and gowns. "I believe it would be best if I saw Lady Seton alone."

"Oh, but Claire," her aunt said, "how would it look if—"

"This isn't a social call, aunt. The woman is coming here to warn me away from her son."

Her aunt and cousin exchanged a look between them. "Then we shall remain and support you."

"Please, I prefer to face her alone. There are things I wish to say, and if you and Ellen are present, I wouldn't be comfortable expressing myself."

* * * *

Harry was shocked yet pleased to learn his mother was paying a call on Claire. He said as much to Claire's aunt and cousin. The way they looked at one another caused prickles of alarm to run down his spine. "Is there something I should know?"

After more looks passing between them, the aunt gestured up the stairs. "My daughter and I were forced to remove ourselves from the vicinity. Perhaps it best if you take your mother home, Lord Seton."

Prickles of alarm turned to dread. Harry took the steps two at a time, and followed the sounds of dissention. He stood outside the door and listened.

* * * *

". . . pray, do not force me—"

"You, Lady Seton, are the one who is no lady. You, my lady, are no better than a bawd!"

"How dare—"

"You admitted you paid your godson to wed me. What do you think that makes you?"

"He made you a lady! I helped you, you ungrateful chit! I gave him funds to ensure the two of you would live comfortably for—"

"Phillip gambled away your money before we arrived in India. Were you so naïve you thought a gamester might actually save his money and not gamble it away?"

Lady Seton looked down her nose at Claire. "A proper wife would have known how—"

"Rubbish! The man was an out and out rotter! When he wasn't seducing anything in skirts, he was gambling with their husbands."

Lady Seton gave an icy smile. "If a man strays, it's because of his wife."

"You are correct, Lady Seton, on that score. I banned Phillip from my bed when we sailed from London." Claire leaned close and winked. "And don't you know," she said in an Irish accent, "he never bothered me once he saw my skain. I always keep it close," she said as she slapped her leg.

Lady Seton stood. "That confirms what I've always known. You'd murder us all in our sleep! Just wait until Harry hears about this!"

Claire rose as well. "Yes, do tell him. Heaven knows I tried last evening."

* * * *

Harry turned when he concluded his mother was taking her leave, and saw the cousin and aunt behind him, their faces grim. "Don't tell her I was here, please," he said before making his way out.

Having his carriage moved so his mother wouldn't see, Harry sat back, still reeling from what he'd heard. Good God, his own mother had maneuvered it all, had paid to have Claire wed to another man. Not just any other man, but Stauton-West! He gave orders to follow his mother's carriage and was relieved she returned home instead of visiting. He didn't think he could contain himself for much longer. As it was, what he had to say wouldn't take very long.

Chapter Seven
Another Heartbreak?

"I'm sorry," Claire said to her aunt and cousin. "I assure you, she won't be returning." Heavens, all she wanted to do was fall on her bed and cry. There was no telling what Lady Seton would tell Harry, but certainly nothing good. "That reminds me. When Lord Seton arrives, extend my apologies, but I couldn't possibly go to the picnic today." Guilt pricked her when Ellen's face fell. "Oh, Ellen, you were so looking forward to attending! I'll—"

"No," Ellen said. "There will be other picnics."

Claire frowned at the look passed between mother and daughter. "What is it?"

"Lord Seton was here earlier," her aunt said. "He stood outside the door and listened."

Claire closed her eyes. "Did he hear me call her a poisoned-tongued harpy?"

"I'm not sure," her aunt replied.

"I believe he began listening when you called her a bawd," Ellen said.

Claire opened her eyes. Really, what did it matter? Hadn't she told him it would never work between them? Now he'd understand. She should be relieved he'd heard. Why then, did it feel like her heart was breaking all over again? "Oh? And did he have any comment?"

Her aunt shook her head. "Said not to tell you he was here."

"I thought he meant his mother," Ellen said.

"It doesn't matter," Claire said. "If you'll excuse me, I think I'll retire to my room." She turned, then stopped. "Oh, bother! I need to send a note to the countess and excuse our absence."

* * * *

Claire waited for the tears to come. Nothing. Just the image of Harry. She thought she'd been careful in guarding her heart, but apparently not. Had some part of her actually believed she and Harry would marry? How pathetic she was. Hadn't she learned ten years ago it was not meant to be?

A knock at her door interrupted her musings.

"A note from Viscount Seton," Ellen said, handing her the missive.

Claire tore the seal and quickly scanned the contents. Her heart shuddered. "He begs our forgiveness. He won't be able to escort us to the picnic after all, but hopes we enjoy ourselves. He says an important matter has arisen that must be attended to immediately."

"Oh, Claire . . ."

Claire could feel the tears coming. "I'd rather be alone, Ellen, if you don't mind." She shut the door in her cousin's face.

* * * *

"Claire," her aunt said through the door, "I strongly urge you to see him. He's most insistent."

Claire sniffed and covered her face with her arm. "I'm in no condition to see anyone. Tell him to come tomorrow afternoon. I plan to leave in the morning."

"Claire," Ellen said, "We really think you should see him. It's not at all what you believed. He wants to see you, to . . . oof!"

Claire raised her arm from her face. "He wants to what?"

"Just come out and you'll see."

"I am in no condition to see anyone." Judging by the way her eyes only opened part way, they were swollen. She knew her face must be red and splotchy. It would take hours for her to look normal.

"Now, Claire," her uncle's voice came from behind the door, "it isn't polite to keep your fi . . . oof!"

Claire looked to the door. Someone's elbow was busy. "I'm not receiving. My eyes are nearly swollen shut. I'm sure I look diseased."

Hearing everyone depart, Claire rose from her bed and looked at her reflection. Worse than she expected. On the bright side, she'd had a wonderful cry and felt the better for it. Or did this sudden lightness of spirit spring from the fact her aunt, uncle and cousin were so insistent she talk to Harry? They wouldn't insist unless they knew she would want to hear what he had to say. She held a cold, wet cloth across her eyes. Perhaps she'd been too precipitous in sending Harry away.

Claire tore the cloth from her eyes and looked at herself in the mirror. She was doing it again. After her confrontation with Lady Seton, how could she allow herself to believe in what could never be?

* * * *

At Claire's aunt's suggestion, Harry returned at nine that evening. He hadn't understood why Claire wouldn't see him until her cousin said she'd been crying. His experience with four sisters, and the aftermath of their tears, cleared the situation. He hoped she would consider herself presentable. He was anxious to get this settled.

Upon seeing Claire's expression when announced, it was evident she didn't expect him. He was at her side before her relatives left the room and holding her hands in his when the door was partially closed.

"Before you answer me," Harry said, "I should tell you I've sent Mother away. She won't be returning." He smiled at her shocked expression. "Did you think there would be no consequences when I discovered what she did? What she did to the both of us?"

"Oh."

"Are you going to cry?" He looked into her tear brimmed eyes. "I thought you'd be gladdened by my announcement."

She nodded, tears running down her cheeks. "I am, truly. But she'll come back. You can't keep her out of town forever."

Harry snorted. "Better than that. I'm keeping her out of the country. She's bound for India. Now, will you marry me, Claire?"

Harry's heart turned over at the sight of Claire's smile.

"Oh, Harry!"

He kept her from throwing her arms around him. "I take that to mean yes. Before we celebrate, allow me to present you with your choice of ring to announce our engagement. They're family heirlooms. This I picked for you ten years ago. But I brought these others so you could compare . . ." He turned when her hand touched his cheek, and saw her lips nearing his. "I suppose we could celebrate now."

"Yes, please. I've waited so long to feel your lips on mine."

Some minutes later, Harry reluctantly pulled away. It was either that or ravish her here and now.

"You will marry me?" he asked as he nibbled her ear. "Soon?"

"Yes. But you must promise to kiss me like this every day."

He chuckled and kissed her hands. "We have years of kissing to catch up on, my love. Days and nights devoted to kissing. That I promise you. He pulled back and looked into her eyes. "I love you, Claire. I always have. It's always been you. Only you." His chest swelled at the sight of her smile.

"I love you as well, Harry. Only and always you."

A Chorus Singing Love

Chapter One
Lady Melody Has a Plan

Melody sat with the invitation pressed to her heart. She'd read it through several times without detecting anything unusual. It appeared to be a straightforward invitation from the Countess of Spode to spend the coming Christmas holiday at Spode Hall.

The wedding last month of Melody's cousin, the Earl of Wickerdun, had brought her to the countess' attention. Doubtless the countess intuited how she avoided all thoughts, all contact with her brother, Trevor Wilde, Earl of Ardmoor. Certainly the countess would have been quick to note how assiduously Trevor avoided *her*. Was that the reason for the invitation? Still pressed against her heart, Melody could detect no ulterior motive in the request for her presence.

Trevor wouldn't have asked his sister to invite Melody. She allowed herself a slight snort. The stubborn man *still* blamed her for the *Unfortunate Incident* of the summer of 1807. Oh, he hadn't said anything to her, he never did, but she'd seen the anger swirling whenever he'd glanced her way. Which had been often. Unquestionably keeping a wary eye on her, making sure she made no untoward advances. Another snort. As if she would ever lower herself to pursue a man, especially him.

Except he is the man I want. The one I've always wanted. The other half of my soul.

Stubborn man! Why couldn't he acknowledge they were meant to be together?

Because he still blames me for the Unfortunate Incident.

Her brother and sister-in-law entered the room.

Melody drew a fortifying breath. "I have been invited by the Countess of Spode to celebrate the Christmas holiday at Spode Hall. I accepted."

Her brother, the Earl of Dore, raised a brow. "The Countess of Spode?" He pursed his lips. "Ardmoor's sister?"

"Yes."

"Is that wise?" he asked softly.

"The Earl of Ardmoor?" Karen, his wife asked. "Oh, but he's missing a leg, Melody. That's not to say you would ever consider marrying him. Not after turning down all the eligible men in the *ton*. He has a wooden peg, you know. "

Melody briefly closed her eyes before turning to her with a smile. "Yes, I'm aware—"

"He lost it in a battle. He's a hero," Karen said. "But still, he's missing a leg." She shuddered. "I can't imagine what being married to a man missing a leg would be like."

Melody believed her. "He may be missing part of his leg, but his soul is still beautiful."

Karen stared at her. "Oh!" she exclaimed. "Did you hear, Dore? Isn't that a lovely sentiment?"

"Were you not on your way to retrieve your needlepoint bag?" Dore asked Karen.

Melody pressed her lips together at Karen's sudden blank expression and turned away, but not before seeing Karen's countenance change to one of purpose.

"Ah! Do excuse me, I meant to retrieve my needlepoint and forgot." Karen left the room.

"Must you manipulate her like that?" Melody snapped. Not that she expected a reply. Dore had married Karen because she was easily manipulated, the result of her blood being completely human, no gifts, no trace of wildness running through her veins. Her brother contended that ever so often those of wild blood needed an infusion of non-wild blood to keep the family lines strong and healthy. Melody couldn't argue with the results—three strapping young sons—but thought he'd have had the strapping young sons no matter whom he'd wed.

"I know you still care for the man," Dore said as soon as the door closed behind Karen. "But he is missing a leg."

"It is not an inheritable trait."

"No, but his inattention, his negligence is. He allowed himself to become vulnerable. You would wed such a man? Breed with him?"

Her brother would be as big a hurdle to overcome as Trevor. She arched her brow. "How can you know what happened? You weren't there. You've heard Ardmoor's praises sung, that his ability, daring and mastery on the battlefield are second to none."

"Yes, our dear brother Hugh near to worships the man, but even he can't explain why Ardmoor allowed himself such an injury."

Melody raised her chin. "Since neither of us has experienced battle with cannon and saber charges, perhaps we're not in a position to judge." She kept her thoughts tightly under control lest he see what had happened that horrible day in Orthez.

Dore's eyes narrowed as if he discerned her involvement. Then he turned away. "I think you're making a mistake. For whatever reason," he said, glancing back at her, "Ardmoor hasn't succumbed. Nor does he look kindly upon you. Never has, not since that summer he visited and all hell broke out." He gave her a wry smile. "Can't say as I blame him."

Melody knew her cheeks were red. "I intend to pursue him. You know I have no other choice." She waited for an objection as she stared at his hands clasped behind his back.

"And after he rejects you? He will, you know. The man has too much pride to yield to you at this point. What then? Will you agree to another Season?" He faced her. "If I allow you this boon, and you fail in your efforts to snag Ardmoor, will you agree to the match I have in mind?"

Melody straightened and encased herself in a cold, soul numbing chill; became a true ice princess. "I will not *snag* Ardmoor. He will propose marriage to me and I shall accept. Therefore, there'll be no need for another ghastly Season, nor marriage, doubtless ungifted as possible, to whomever you've selected for me."

* * * *

"I expect you're not used to being entertained in the nursery," the Countess of Spode said with a large smile.

Melody shook her head. Other than the nursery at Bruin Tor, she didn't think she'd ever been in a child's nursery. As rooms went it was rather cheerful, with large paintings adorning the ceiling and walls. Paintings of Dennene, Shenti, wood nymphs and other folk if she wasn't mistaken. Little Lord Raker appeared amused by the life-sized figures as he toddled around the room, touching the walls and laughing.

"I enjoy my son's company and once the other guests arrive, I shall be forced to spend most of my time with them. I knew I could bring you up here and not have to answer any awkward questions about the paintings."

Melody's gaze swung to the countess. Only kindness and understanding showed on her face. Melody struggled for the right thing to say. Too often her responses were received as cold or arrogant.

"Thank you, Countess." She watched her reaction, then lifted the corners of her mouth at the countess' warm smile.

"Maddy, if you please. Actually,"—Maddy picked up her son and held him on her lap—"I had an ulterior motive in inviting you to arrive before the other guests."

Melody ignored the thoughts swarming from the woman. "You wrote that you hoped to further our acquaintance."

"Well, yes. I was curious about you. You see, my brother, Ardmoor, had the most peculiar reaction around you when we attended Wickerdun's wedding at Fairhills. A sort of fascination he was loath to admit. As if . . ."

Melody's hands covered her face. "Because he does loathe me. Ever since the *Unfortunate Incident of the summer of '07.*"

* * * *

"What unfortunate incident?" Robert Baideson, Earl of Spode asked, his mind picturing numerous scenarios. "Sounds scandalous."

"She said she promised Ardmoor never to speak of it," Maddy replied.

"Oh." He made a face when Maddy laughed. "Well, in light of this, do you think it wise to continue? After all, if he loathes her, I don't see much success in a match coming about."

"He doesn't loathe her," Maddy said. "He is drawn to her, but doesn't want to be so he fights it—something I've never witnessed with him. I think this will be a jolly spectacle watching the two of them come together."

Spode didn't know who to pity more: his brother-in-law or Lady Melody. "If you say so, dearest."

* * * *

The sudden warm burn at her core announced his arrival. Melody sat straighter when she heard his voice. She rubbed her moist palms on her gown. Would he enter the drawing room or go straight to his chamber? Was her hair neat? Should she have worn this gown? Why, oh why, had she accepted the invitation? Then she heard him say he'd brought a guest.

She watched Maddy glide to the door and quickly close it behind her. The temptation to listen in on the conversation beyond the door proved great, but Melody knew better. Was Maddy informing her brother of her presence? Would he leave?

* * * *

Ardmoor didn't like the smile on his brother-in-law's face. He and Major Hugh Bruin, his guest, stood in the great hall. "What's so bloody amusing?" He turned as his sister emerged. "Why is your husband grinning like a fool?" His eyes narrowed when she gasped at the sight of his guest.

"How lovely! You've brought Major Bruin!" Maddy said.

Ardmoor saw the look pass between Maddy and Spode. "What the devil—"

Maddy broke in. "You'll be pleased to know cousin Victor is enjoying the holiday with us as well. All these military folk. Just the thing for all the ladies invited," she said gaily.

He wasn't fooled. "Maddy, you and Spode aren't planning any matchmaking are you?"

"Hold on." Hugh walked to the drawing room door. "Is . . ." He stopped at the door as if suddenly recalling his hosts and turned back. "Ah," he said and smiled, rocking on his heels.

Ardmoor looked at the closed door and cocked his head. The tightening in his groin announced who was inside.

Bypassing the drawing room, he strode straight to his chambers. He stood at the window and stared sightlessly out at the lawn. The fury he felt went deep; was old. Once again she was back in his life.

He should have told Maddy the truth of it long ago. She'd not have invited her. No, she'd have invited some other woman. What the bloody hell did Maddy think she was doing? If his sister thought she would achieve a match this Christmas season, she was sadly off her mark. What the bloody hell was Spode about to allow his wife free rein to ruin a man's holiday? "Gutless, bloody bastard."

"My lord?" Watkins asked.

Ardmoor turned, saw the ribbon in his man's hand and frowned.

"My lord." Watkins knelt before Ardmoor's peg. "You promised Miss Joy you'd wear her ribbons. The little mite said she's made a wish on each ribbon, and made me swear I'd see you wore them. If you'll stick your peg—"

"Just tie the bloody thing on," Ardmoor muttered. Who knew what foul wishes his niece might have imbued upon the ribbons? He glared down at the pink bow. Indeed, his niece's wishes were potent. Especially around Christmas. Last year she got the new mother she'd wished for. What might have she wished for him? He shuddered. "I don't suppose she told you what she wished, did she?"

"Bloody, bloody hell."

Chapter Two
Ardmoor Fumes and Wonders

Relief swept over him to see Melody seated at the opposite end of the table, at Spode's right. Ardmoor took his seat on his sister's right. Unfortunately, no obstructions blocked Melody from his sight. Surely it was the *curse of '07*, for his attention kept wandering to her end of the table, and inevitably to her.

She looked like she was enjoying herself. Same as at the wedding. Quite unlike her cold self when amongst the *ton*. The ice princess he'd heard her called. Odd, given she was presumably trying to snare a husband. He bit back a grin recalling his friend Doune's brief encounter and courtship with Melody, and the man's conviction his willy would freeze and break off if he ever bedded her. Didn't she know men didn't like ice princesses?

Of course she knew that.

Then why the bloody hell did she attend every Season if she obviously had no intention of accepting any man's proposal? Bloody waste of time and money.

She looked as lovely as ever. Light blonde hair—almost white—with strands of silver and gold running through. He'd never come upon the like since meeting her, so he assumed it came from her wild blood. She knew how to wear a gown with effect, he'd allow her that. Not that he knew about fashion, but he'd overheard women nattering on about her. Or perhaps her dressmaker and maid knew how to dress her. One would never guess she was six-and-twenty, seven years his junior. Her gown's décolleté plunged unusually low, not that he cared, her bosom almost entirely exposed. Was Dore aware of her dressing style? Well, if she wanted to flaunt herself he didn't care. Except one could see just about everything, couldn't one? Were her breasts that firm or was it some contraption pushing them up like an offering?

Ardmoor scowled. Her hand rested on cousin Victor's hand. A vivid image of a woman, no, a ballet dancer sprang from his cousin's mind. Ah, so she was advising him on his love life. Ardmoor snorted and drained his wine glass. Like asking a bloody farmer how to sail a boat.

Ardmoor sat straighter. Why was she here? Why did she accept Maddy's invitation? She didn't still harbor matrimonial hopes toward him, did she? Surely she knew better than that.

* * * *

Melody looked to see who else had heard Trevor's thoughts as they preceded his entrance to the dining hall, and saw several grinning. Warmth rushed from her core to her throat at the sight of his handsome face. Lowering her eyes before he caught her staring, she wondered if the sight of her still caused him to become aroused. Judging by his actions, one would think one look at her had the opposite effect. Odd as it was, his presence had a calming effect on her—always had. After all, he *was* the other half of her soul.

Melody noted how often Trevor looked her way, sometimes staring at her. His expression wasn't especially pleasant. She sighed. If she could get him alone and talk to him . . . But no, he avoided coming anywhere near her. If he would listen to her, allow her to explain, and hear her apology. *Apologies*, she amended. Didn't he understand they were both caught? Had been since the summer of '07. Ten years ago. The stubborn man would doubtless choose to go to his grave unwed rather than marry her.

Did he have a mistress? Was he able? Melody was incapable of passion with other men. Over the years she'd tried kissing a few, but felt nothing. But a rare sight of Trevor and immediately her blood raced. Possibly men could overcome the single-minded lust induced by the wood nymph's song.

He would have to wed eventually though, he knew his duty. He *was* an earl.

Melody drew her gaze away from his face. He was more handsome than when they'd first met. Auburn hair worn longer since leaving the army, it curled just over his collar and around his ears. His eyes the same deep green as his sister's, and doubtless as mesmerizing as she remembered, judging by how often Maddy's husband was seen gazing into her eyes. A small scar marred his square jaw on the right, but Melody viewed it as a badge of honor. Unfortunately, her father had given it to him. His lips . . . ah, to kiss him again.

However, if she wanted to kiss him she'd have to talk to him first. Which meant getting him alone. Which he would avoid like the plague.

Did that mean he feared what he might do if alone with her? Melody smiled. *If* he were still as aroused by her as he once was, then of course he'd avoid her. Especially since he'd never forgiven her for the *Unfortunate Incident*. But no, she needed him listening to her, not lusting after her. Heavens, if she tricked him by using his lust, he'd never forgive her! She needed a way to make him listen while keeping them a safe distance apart.

* * * *

Ardmoor followed the men to the drawing room, pausing at the door to reconnoiter. He wouldn't put it past his sister to swoop upon him and forcibly lead him next to Melody. But no, Melody sat next to the elderly Lady Susan, both chatting quietly. It looked safe enough. The other ladies were either conversing together or already claimed. His usual comfortable chair in a far corner was unoccupied. He nearly made his way without incident before Lady Susan requested he join her and explain to Lady Melody about the horse he'd given her.

"Analayan, was it not?" she asked.

He maintained a safe distance and glared at the two women. "Andalusian. From Spain." With a bow he retreated to his dark corner, gritting his teeth upon hearing their laughter. The old bat was aware of his predicament, he knew it.

The rest of the evening passed uneventfully. Conversation flowed, the piano played, songs sung, card tables set up and used. He sat tight, watching, waiting for his sister to make her move. It came when tea was poured. He saw Maddy send Melody with his cup, but he waved her away before she got too close.

"We must talk," Melody said softly.

"No, we don't," he replied. He must have glared, for she took a step back. She raised her chin, compressed her lips and squared her shoulders before giving him a stony stare. Then she pirouetted and walked away.

When it was apparent the evening was at an end, he escaped. Without stopping, he saluted his sister as he stomped by and mumbled a general good-night to all assembled. He ignored any replies.

Later, he wondered what the bloody hell she thought they had to talk about?

Ardmoor swirled his brandy and leaned his head back against the chair. He was in Spode's library, because that's where Spode kept the good stuff. All were asleep, or so he hoped. He was in no mood for idle conversation.

He would leave in the morning. Obviously he couldn't remain, not with her here. Though he'd maintained his distance, her presence affected him. If he stayed, he'd be a babbling idiot by the time Christmas arrived. Or, God help him, betrothed to her. Ever aware he'd never be able to wed another woman and retain his sanity, damned if he'd accede to her after all these years. A surge of anger shot through him as he considered the state to which she'd reduced him, and his fingers tightened around the glass.

Bloody, thoughtless bitch.

Chapter Three
Lady Melody Amazes

Melody closed her eyes upon hearing his words. Although spoken silently, they pertained to her. She hesitated. No, they needed to talk and if he wouldn't agree, then she would have to force him to listen to her. She hoped it wouldn't come to that, for it would undoubtedly be noisy and she didn't want everyone awakened.

The library was dark when she opened the door. A loud, martyred sigh escaped her lips as she locked the door behind her. She lighted the lamp on the desk and other candles so they could see one another, then shoved a table against the door—sure such an act would elicit a reaction from him.

"What the devil do you think you're doing?" He emerged from behind a curtain.

She shivered at the near growl of his voice. "We need to talk. I want..."

He pointed his cane at her. "No, as *I* said before, we don't. You still don't listen."

Melody nearly backed down. His anger was potent, nearly sending her to her knees in shame. Then she remembered her mission. "But we—"

"Surely you know the consequences if we remain together for much longer." His sudden smile was unpleasant. "Is that what you want? Is that the reason you sought me out in the dark of night, alone, pushing a bl-blasted table against the door? Is that to keep me in or others out? Tell me. Tell me what you want."

"Stop!" When he continued to advance she pulled the pistol from her pocket. Relief filled her when he halted. Then he smiled another disagreeable smile.

"Will you shoot me if I don't? Do you think my death will ease your longing for me? It won't. You'll still be cursed by—"

"Of course I wouldn't shoot you! Don't you realize how much I suffered when you lost your leg? The pain I felt? The anguish? I felt it all, Trevor. Every bit of it. Even the year you spent in a drunken haze, I felt it all."

He arched a brow, his lips turned down. "Then you must feel how angry I am at the moment. I suggest you put the pistol away. Better yet, give it to me."

He didn't believe her. She shook her head. "No, I won't shoot you, but I'll shoot your peg. I'll shoot it right off, I promise you!"

"You—"

"It's the only threat I have to get you to listen to me and make sure the lust doesn't overtake you." His eyes bugged as he looked from her to the pistol. "I've given this much thought and threatening your peg seemed to be the surest way to get you to listen. Have a seat over there and I'll sit here. With my pistol pointed at your peg."

"You—"

"Please, Trevor." She winced at the tremor in her voice. He'd sneer at any softness heard, thinking it a ruse. After a narrow-eyed glare at the pistol, he made his way to a chair and sat.

"Start talking." He leaned forward with his cane positioned between his legs. "As soon as I'm over the shock, I'll likely strangle you. Not for the sheer effrontery of threatening to shoot off my peg, which is unbelievably colossal, but because you're responsible for the peg to begin with!"

Melody stared. "*I* caused it? *You* called out to me!"

"I most certainly did not! Your image came to me, and the next thing I knew we—I went flying off my horse. Not content with that, you tried to drag me into The Shadow!"

"I was saving you! I saved your horse! At least he was intelligent enough to seek safety!"

She leaned forward when he didn't speak. She wished the room were brighter so she could see his expression.

"So that's how he survived," Ardmoor said softly.

"I didn't seek you out, truly. But when you called to me, naturally I answered."

"Hmm. Something to puzzle out in my declining years, for I never called to you. Begin talking." He waved at her to continue.

"I apologize for the *Unfortunate Incident* of the summer of '07. But I'm not admitting I did it on purpose." She leaned back, the darkness of his anger nearly touching her.

"You still can't admit it?"

His wrath was palpable. Her ordered thoughts fled. "Yes, I admit I caused it, but I didn't realize what I was doing! All I knew was I recognized in you the man who was the other half of my soul. The man I should marry. I admit I spoke to the wood nymphs, and asked for their assistance, but I didn't realize what would happen. No one had ever—"

"I told you then you were too young." He stood. "I said to wait until you'd come out, and then we'd talk if you still felt the same. I explained your family wouldn't agree to your wedding a military man, a second son. But no, you decided you wanted me, and the bloody hell with propriety and convention! You were sixteen, by God! It didn't matter to you what *I* wanted. No, you ignored my wishes, my wants and proceeded to get me nearly killed! Not to mention the years *both* of us have suffered."

"I admit I was wrong, but the truth is still there, Trevor! You're the other half of my soul. I can't function—"

"Enough!" he snapped as he slashed the air with his cane. "More than enough, actually," he said in a quieter tone. "You and I are cursed with the *gift* you thought to bestow. But hear me well, Lady Melody, for I shall say it plain and for the last time. What you did in order to have us wed was the worst sort of trickery, something I won't forgive, nor forget. You and I shall never marry."

She watched him stride past, roughly shove the table aside, unlock the door and exit the room. "I still love you," she said. But he was long gone.

* * * *

"Waiting for a gunshot?" Spode asked his wife as they lay in bed.

"Yes," Maddy replied. "Or screaming. Not that I think Melody will be forced to shoot." She frowned at her husband's chuckle. Really, this wasn't at all humorous.

"By Jupiter, I do wish I could see Ardmoor's face when she whips out the pistol and threatens to blow off his peg." He laughed harder.

Maddy rolled her eyes. "I hope it works. I believe he'd be happy with her. I wish I knew what the unfortunate incident was that precipitated their breach."

"We may never know. You do realize it will take Ardmoor several days to get over his anger at the fact he was held at gunpoint with the threat of losing his peg, don't you?"

Maddy yawned. "No, he has another. If I know Watkins, the man has several in reserve; he's very efficient."

"Not the point. Your brother has a peg because he lost his leg in battle. Most men would feel less than a man because they have a wooden leg; I'm sure I would. Lady Melody comes along, a woman he doesn't appear to like, and she threatens his weakness. I don't think Ardmoor's mood will be pleasant tomorrow."

Maddy scowled. "No, I believe Ardmoor accepts his loss. It took him near a year in bed with great quantities of brandy, but he came to his senses." She smiled at her husband. "I believe it was you, when you sought him out to ask permission to wed me that made him realize it was time to get on with his life."

"So I should be rewarded for my good deed?"

"Yes, my love, you should."

* * * *

After Watkins divested him of his coat, Ardmoor sent him away and sat in a large chair near the fire grate. He didn't want to talk, didn't want to hear Watkins' observations about the guests and their servants. He did learn Melody rode every morning, so he would ride in the afternoon as part of his avoidance strategy. Then recalled he meant to tell Watkins to pack, that he intended to leave. But where would he go? The thought of spending Christmas alone on one of his estates wasn't appealing. Nor was the thought of intruding upon his friends. He knew he'd be welcomed, but Christmas was meant to be celebrated with family.

Shoot my peg off, would she? Ha! Keeping that threat foremost when in her presence should certainly cool his ardor. His thoughts drifted, and her words repeated themselves until he shut them out. He lifted his right leg, pulling off the pink ribbon. The bloody leg that wasn't there ached like hell's fire.

* * * *

It certainly hadn't gone as she'd planned. Her eloquent apology and explanation wasn't remembered until he'd gone. Melody didn't know how she could face him. But she would, it was inevitable. Maddy said he rode in the morning, so she would put off her ride until he returned. Possibly she wouldn't see him until later in the day. By then she might have some idea of what to do, how to proceed when she encountered him. How did one react to such dislike? Not just dislike, but rejection.

Anger toward her she could understand, but so much anger seemed out of proportion to her transgression. He rarely let a thought slip by to help her along and she didn't dare try to slip in and peek.

Despite her wants, the stubborn man refused to listen, refused to consider taking her as wife. Heavens, he didn't want to be in the same room with her! He'd made it quite plain there would be no wedding between them, and she didn't foresee him changing his mind. Which meant she needed to go forward with her own plans for her future.

Then the throbbing in her leg started. She rubbed, knowing the quicker she eased the discomfort she felt, the sooner Trevor's agony would be relieved. Obviously the stubborn man didn't seek anyone's help with his pain. She should have pointed out one of the advantages of marriage to her would be a wife to ease his physical aches and pains.

Chapter Four
Ardmoor Antagonizes

"I thought you rode in the morning," Ardmoor said from the doorway of the breakfast room. His sudden arousal should have alerted him she was near.

"I could say the same," Melody replied. "My intention was to avoid you, which, it would appear, was your intention."

He hesitated entering since she was the only guest present, but he'd appear craven by turning away. He walked in and sat across from her, looking for tell-tale signs of a night spent weeping because of his rejection. Her complexion was as fair as ever. He grunted at the thought of her crying over anyone. *The Ice Princess.* Why the bloody hell did she still want to marry him?

Melody set down her fork and knife, arching a delicate, blonde brow at him. "You're not eating?"

Ardmoor looked at the food on the sideboard and the two footmen waiting at attention. Damned if he'd rise to show a bloody maypole in his trousers. He motioned for a plate to be brought to him. He glanced back at Melody, but she quickly looked away, giving her full attention to her food. Why was her face flushed? He stopped himself from smacking his head. Of course! She felt as aroused in his presence as he felt in hers.

He couldn't help grinning upon realizing the potential mayhem he could cause her. No, that would be cruel. He moved to allow his plate to be placed before him. Except she *had* threatened to shoot his peg. He took a sip of coffee and gently placed the cup onto the saucer.

"*Would you care to ride with me?*" he asked silently. Her knife and fork clattered onto the table. She looked up and he clearly saw hope in her eyes before realization set in. Guilt flitted briefly in his mind. *No! Her family nearly killed me because of what she did.* He smirked. Then arched his brows when she tossed her napkin onto the table as she rose. "Not finishing your tea?" A brief image from her of his head drenched with tea made him smile.

"I believe I shall ride with my brother," she huffed before exiting the room.

* * * *

After racing, they walked their horses, stopping atop a hill. It had been a pleasant surprise to see her brother Hugh as a guest. "How did you come to be invited?" she asked.

Hugh smiled. "As you may be aware, I'm on half-pay at the moment, with nowhere I need to be. For whatever reason, Ardmoor sought me out a few weeks ago, after Wickerdun's wedding. Since he's aware of my aversion to Bruin Tor, or rather, Dore, he invited me as a guest. I gladly accepted."

"He sought you out?" Melody asked. Was Trevor seeking a connection to her through her brother? No, more likely he was ensuring she had no plans concerning him.

They sat silently enjoying the countryside, then Hugh asked how the conquest of Ardmoor was going.

"He despises me."

Hugh laughed. "I doubt that. He hasn't turned tail and run. Although he may despise the fact you've taken away the choice of wife from him."

Melody stared at him. "Taken away his choice of wife? I'd never considered my actions in quite that light before, but . . . I did though, didn't I? Is that why he's so angry?"

Hugh shrugged. "I'd be angry."

"But he's the other half of my soul! He—Don't roll your eyes at me!"

"Melly, I've heard that for the past ten years, and I want to retch each time I hear it said. How can he be your other half? Were you born with only half a soul? Are you walking around with only half a soul? Is he?" He sighed when he saw tears rolling down her cheeks. "I'm sorry, Melly, don't cry, it's just—"

"I suppose Trevor feels the same way. It's no use. The stubborn man is so full of anger toward me he'll never come around."

"Well, given time I'm sure he—"

"Don't try to placate me, it's been ten years. I'm already considered an ape-leader. I'll be withered and barren by the time he comes to his senses. Then I'll be too old to marry." She wiped her eyes with the heel of her glove. "Dore has someone picked out for me."

Hugh winced. He could imagine the sort Dore would chose for her. "Sorry."

"Don't be sorry. I have a plan." She looked at him with a weak smile. "Since I couldn't be sure Trevor would listen to me I knew I needed a plan in reserve."

Her tears were gone, but replaced with a determined look Hugh didn't like. "What kind of plan? You can't thwart Dore, he's head of the family." His concern wasn't eased at the sight of her smile.

Once back at the stable, Hugh said, "No! You can't, Melly. Dore would confine you if he knew! Nor do I think it wise. Questions raised, you know that. Our kind would get all exercised. No, it'll never work."

Melody laughed. "It has worked. And Lady Susan said she thought it a wonderful way for me to survive on my own."

"Yes, I'm sure she did. Has she made mention of her blue unicorn to you yet? Melly, you can't . . ." He muttered a curse when his sister strode away.

* * * *

Ardmoor watched Melody and Hugh approach from the stable. Hugh looked to be arguing with her, and even from this distance Ardmoor could tell she'd put up a shield. Her ice shield. He arched his brows in surprise. So it wasn't natural, but something she erected for protection.

Why the bloody hell was she shielding herself from Hugh? Obviously she'd angered her brother. Possibly threatened to shoot something of *his* off.

Ardmoor positioned himself so she'd see him upon entering. At first thinking to agitate her, he decided it would be more amusing to do nothing and see her reaction. He blinked when she sailed past with a curt nod in his direction. He stared after her, then became aware of Hugh's agitation behind him. The man was pulling on his hair. Ardmoor caught some of the thoughts flying wide and grabbed Hugh, tugging him outside.

"She *what?*" Ardmoor exclaimed.r Surely he'd misunderstood.

"She wants to work with the magistrates to apprehend murderers and thieves."

"She can't—"

"I told her that! Then she encased herself and wouldn't listen. It's my fault. I shouldn't have made fun of her *half of my soul* drivel. It made her cry."

"She cries?" Difficult to imagine her crying. "What do you mean, drivel? Sounds rather poetic. Not that I feel the same way she does, of course."

Hugh paced. "Dore will . . . I don't know what Dore will do. Melly says he has someone selected for her, which I believe is the reason she's determined on this crazed plan of hers."

"Dore always has a suitor lined up for her," Ardmoor said. "She manages to repel them. Or so I've been told."

"She *thinks* she can outsmart him," Hugh continued. "She doesn't realize how gifted he is, or how ruthless. Not to mention if others found out what she was doing . . ."

"Yes," Ardmoor snapped. "Which is why this conversation goes no further. Surely the two of us can persuade her how dangerous this foolish idea of hers is."

Hugh shook his head. "Lady Susan knows. Melly said she encouraged her."

Ardmoor cursed. No doubt he'd have to gift the old bat another Andalusian to ensure her silence.

Chapter Five
A Missive Breaks the Ice

"You're just in time!" Maddy said brightly. "I'm trying to get a group together to gather greens for our indoor Christmas decorations."

"Bit of rain," Ardmoor said.

Hugh snuck away when Maddy opened the door to check.

"Nonsense." Maddy closed the door. "Will you and Major Bruin . . . Where did he get to? Well, would you care to join us?"

He lifted a brow. *Not bloody likely.* "No. Where's Lady Susan?"

"In the drawing room, I believe. But gathering greens is a traditional—"

"Perhaps another time" Ardmoor headed for the drawing room.

"Of course I shan't tell anyone," Lady Susan declared after he'd discussed Melody's plans with her. She set her needlework aside and looked at him with a smug smile.

"It would be awkward for Lady Melody should word get out."

"Oh, I agree," Lady Susan said. "Dangerous as well."

"Then why did you encourage her?"

"The girl needed encouragement. *Some* people could be a little nicer to her, you know. *Some* people might try to understand her fears."

Ardmoor clenched his jaw.

"*Some* people—"

"She threatened to shoot off my peg!" He scowled when Lady Susan broke into laughter.

"Did she? Oh my, but that's—"

"Cut line," Ardmoor growled. "Another Andalusian for your silence?"

Lady Susan nodded. "That would be lovely. A female this time, I think. Ricco should like a mate, don't you agree?"

Ardmoor closed the drawing room door behind him. Right. One female Andalusian to purchase. Who knew what color the old bat would dye this one. Now to find Melody.

"Oh, now are you free to join us?" Maddy asked as she glided his way.

Ardmoor looked for the group she spoke of, but the hall was empty. Doubtless all fled when she turned her attention to him. "No. Where is Lady Melody?" His eyes narrowed when she clapped her hands together, gave a hop and smiled. "Don't get your hopes raised. I simply need to talk to her."

"Of course you do. I'm so happy to hear you and she are talking."

"Until I find her, we won't be talking, Maddy."

"She's in her room."

"Will you get her for me?"

"Will you help us gather greens?"

"I think not." He moved past her.

Not until his hand rested on the rail did Ardmoor realize he couldn't wait outside Melody's chamber door without causing talk. His eyes narrowed. Was that what this was all about? Merely a ruse to get him close to her? Had Hugh . . . No, he'd been genuinely horrified at his sister's avowed intention. But had Melody carefully crafted her words to cause Hugh to come to him?

Was this another trap? Or was Melody serious about pursuing murderers and thieves? His gut clenched at the thought of her in harm's way. Bloody, thoughtless minx! Didn't she know how . . .? He'd wait to talk to her. She wasn't going anywhere. In fact, he'd observe her before doing any talking, possibly take a look inside her . . . no, that would be dangerous, too close for his comfort.

Instead he'd visit Spode and see if the man were missing a pistol. Heels clacked on the floor behind him, and he turned to face his sister.

"Didn't you find Lady Melody?"

"Haven't looked. It can wait." He nearly laughed at her disappointed expression.

"Oh. Well in that case, you should help with gathering greens for house decorations. We'll be leaving shortly."

Ardmoor blew out a breath. "Maddy, the ground is wet. My peg leg doesn't handle the sodden ground well. Sinks in and I fall. Much as it distresses me to be unable to join you, I believe it best if I remain inside."

"Oh." She looked down at his peg and then to his eyes. "Oh. But you've always . . . I never realized . . . I never thought . . . oh, I am sorry, Ardmoor."

He closed his eyes and nodded. "Don't give it another thought."

As she hurried away, Spode came striding past to join her. Ardmoor blocked his way, standing with his hands fisted on his hips, he stared at Spode. "Did you give her the pistol?"

Spode stopped in his tracks and winced. "I did. It wasn't loaded, though."

"But I didn't know that!"

"I suggested it might not be the wisest plan, but Maddy talked me into it."

"Gutless bas—"

"No, not gutless," Spode said, clearly serious, "just in love with my wife. Because of my hesitation in pursuing Maddy, six years of our lives as man and wife were wasted. I treasure each day, each moment we share. And I trust her judgment. I would grant her anything, Ardmoor, anything. Sneer if you will, but when you decide to choose your countess I trust you'll understand. Now if you'll excuse me, I promised to join my wife in gathering greenery. Will you be joining us?"

"No." Ardmoor retreated to the library, searching for a newspaper he hadn't already read. Hearing voices outside, he ambled to the window to see Maddy and Spode leading a large group of people. Melody walked among them.

"Bloody hell." He wasn't sure if he was relieved he hadn't participated, or regretted it. And that conundrum left him puzzling for an answer.

* * * *

"Oh dear," Melody whispered. "Oh, what have I done!" *How could I have been so wrong?*

Maddy patted her arm. "You didn't know. If I'd had the slightest niggle he was so sensitive about his peg, I never—"

"But I should have known!" Melody cried. And she claimed he was the other half of her soul? If that was true she should have been aware of the restrictions it placed upon him, his sensitivity regarding his wooden peg. Instead, she'd intuited the opposite. "Oh, I should have known." She covered her eyes and shook her head. "I never do anything right when it comes to him!"

* * * *

After observing the group, Melody in particular, for as long as they remained in view, Ardmoor sat with a glass of brandy. Why, he asked himself, and very quietly too considering some of the guests present, why did the sight of Melody walking with the others, her arms dripping with vegetation, make him want to leap out and join them? As much as he wanted to place the blame at her door for such an extraordinary notion, he knew it was nothing she'd done.

Was it the season? Christmas *was* the only time of year he regretted not having wife and family. Perhaps his niece's wishes? Or the gutless bastard's remark about granting his wife anything she wanted? Another extraordinary notion. How could the man admit such a thing? Yet he knew Spode and knew the man spoke true. He *would* grant his wife anything. The more Ardmoor thought about it, the more brandy he consumed, the more novel the concept became—and more appealing.

He woke with a start, thinking he'd heard singing. For a horrible, panic-stricken moment he thought the wood nymphs were at it again, and his body prepared to flee. Then he realized the singing came from the music room. With no desire to be snagged into singing Christmas songs, he decided his chamber would be safe.

Ardmoor stared at the missive Watkins held before him.

"From Lady Melody, my lord. Her maid delivered it."

Ardmoor held it with his thumb and forefinger. It reeked of apology and sadness. He let it fall upon his desk and wiped his hands. Now what? Why the bloody hell had she written?

"I'll have my bath now." Ardmoor gave his back to the letter, but it was no use. He had to know what she'd written to cause such angst. He turned and grabbed the thing, breaking the seal. One glance showed this wasn't a one liner setting up an assignation, but two full sheets. He sat and read every word, then re-read it. By the time his bath was ready and he was nude, he'd read it a third time.

She'd apologized: For threatening to shoot his peg; for taking his choice of wife away from him; for inducing the wood nymph lust in him—although she still insisted she hadn't been aware that *that* was the consequence of the song she'd requested—and she apologized for ruining his life.

He was surprised she hadn't apologized for the Great War against Napoleon.

Using a stool to support and steady his amputated leg, he entered the tub and waved Watkins away. Leaning against the back of the tub, he raised his right leg. He was used to the stump, but couldn't imagine a woman looking at it without shrieking and fainting dead away. Although Maddy had tended to him when he returned home and she hadn't fainted, had she? But she was his sister. As best he could remember, she'd been more inclined to nag him about his drinking.

Certainly a lady wouldn't want it to touch her. He lay back and closed his eyes. How would it be possible to have marital relations without his stump coming into contact with his wife? Although myriad positions were possible, there were few suitable for a wedding night with an innocent woman. One, really, for a virgin. Certainly a lady wouldn't want it to touch her. He groaned.

And why the bloody hell had he allowed his thoughts to veer in this direction?

When he saw her, he needed to assure her she hadn't offended him. Maddy must have put the bee in her bonnet about his alleged sensitivity regarding his peg. The rest of the letter would go unmentioned. That would be best.

Chapter Six
Ardmoor Astounds

Melody's mouth hung open. She stared at Trevor, wondering if she'd heard correctly. He'd requested a moment of her time, if she was agreeable. His green eyes held no malice, no laughter at her expense. "Of course," she replied.

He led her to a settee, stopped and then changed direction, leading her to a pair of chairs.

Melody sat, breathing in his clean scent. She tingled, was aware he wasn't angry, knew he wanted to discuss the letter, worried if her want for him was evident, whether he noticed her gown, if he liked it, and wondered when she'd calm herself enough to hear and understand him. She smiled and smoothed the gown with her fingers.

"It was unnecessary for you to apologize to me about my wooden peg. I've grown accustomed to the thing. Although I didn't appreciate your threat to shoot it off, I can, now that time has passed, see a certain humor in the situation."

Melody's face heated. "I'm sorry—"

"It was a remarkable attempt at coercion. I applaud you."

It astounded Melody to see a twinkle in his eyes, no matter how briefly. "You applaud me?"

"Yes, but be aware a second attempt will be frowned upon and dealt with severely."

Her face heated again and she looked down at her lap. "There won't be a second attempt. As I wrote in the letter—"

"Yes, well, just be assured I'm not sensitive where my peg is concerned."

"But Maddy said you—"

"I fobbed her off because I didn't want to go tromping about plucking at perfectly innocent greenery all afternoon. She wouldn't take no for an answer, so I resorted to other tactics."

Melody nodded as the knowledge of what he said sunk in. She hadn't insulted him!

"Are we clear about that issue?"

She smiled and nodded, drinking in his handsome face, the green of his eyes. He'd bathed not long ago. And been shaved again, too. Sandalwood wafted in the air. When Trevor wore sandalwood she wanted to press her face against his neck and breathe him in. Among other things.

"You were actually perceptive when you described how I felt about my peg. How did you know?"

She almost replied because he was the other half of her soul, but recalled her brother's derisive opinion on the matter. With the assumption he felt the same, she said, "I want you to know I've never entered your mind. We were raised to know better. Before the *Unfortunate Incident,* you used to let thoughts slip through. When that happened I caught them, and was comforted, because it was as if your thoughts and mine fit together, like two hands joined together; it strengthened me. As I became more adept at catching your thoughts, I used to try to anticipate them. Before long I could catch them as they formed. Then, too, I'm fairly gifted at seeing a person's shimmer, the aura I believe some call it, and there's much useful information to be . . ." She stopped when she saw his frown. "I never entered, really, I never did.

"After the *Unfortunate Incident,* you never let any thoughts through. It was only certain times when they would come to me, I assume times when you were under duress. When they did come it was easy to gather much information from the little that escaped. I found that after the *Unfortunate Incident* I became more attuned to you physically. I knew when you were hungry, tired, happy or sad. I smelled the smells around you, could taste what pleased and displeased you. I felt your pain when your leg was hit, when it was removed. I know when your missing leg aches, for I feel the pain, too."

"You feel the pain?" he asked sharply.

Melody nodded. "When that happens I rub the pain away for you." He inhaled sharply and sat back. Bother! She hadn't meant to reveal that. Really, why did she always lose her wits around him? "So that's how I knew how you felt about your peg." He stared at her, his face solemn. She plucked at her gown, the temptation growing to see what he was thinking the longer he remained silent. She knew he would never offer for her, he'd made that plain, but was it possible he might not continue to hold her in contempt?

Relief flooded Melody when dinner was announced. Trevor still hadn't said anything to her.

"We'll talk more after dinner." He stood and offered his arm.

Melody smiled, and warmth swept her body. If he wanted to continue talking, then perhaps that meant...

"I want to hear about the dangerous and unsuitable endeavor your brother complained to me about."

An image of Hugh and Trevor joined against her burst into her head. She swallowed a groan from the effort of pulling back from him. "I don't believe I care to discuss that with you, Ardmoor."

* * * *

Ardmoor stared after Melody, his eyes following the gentle sway of her hips. He *had* noticed her gown and he *did* like it on her. Aside from the fact she acted repulsed at the thought of touching his arm—which was ludicrous since the two of them were under a constant compulsion to come together—and she'd been angered at his presumption to question her intended plan of action—something was different, unsettling about their parting. Not until he sat at the table had he realized what it was.

She'd called him Ardmoor! He further realized she'd been calling him Trevor all along. How could he have not noticed? He stared at her, saw her actually shield herself from *him*, then glared at his soup. Minx! *Had* he noticed she used his Christian name? Noticed, yet—for whatever reason—chose not to correct her? What the devil? He glared at her.

* * * *

Melody felt his attention. As often and as long as she'd wished for such . . . well, something other than a hostile stare . . . she was unprepared for its intensity. She'd shielded herself, but could tell when he looked her way. Except for Dore, she'd never come across one so powerful. If Trevor ever looked upon her with favor, she'd doubtless expire from the experience. She hoped none of the other guests were aware of what was transpiring, for it would be too embarrassing. Except, she scolded herself, nothing was really happening. He was simply looking at her. Intently. Intently with eyes not completely full of disfavor. He'd never done that before. It was impossible to eat. She had to get hold of herself.

When the ladies withdrew, Melody didn't know whether to remain in the drawing room or claim a headache and retire to her chamber. It was cowardly to evade him, yet she knew what he intended to say. But Maddy appeared at her side, gripped her arm and led her to the settee.

Maddy smiled. "You and Ardmoor spoke?"

Melody nodded. "We talked. Then he intruded into a private area. So perhaps I should leave before the men return." Maddy gripped her arm, forcing her to remain seated.

"Nonsense! You can't avoid him altogether, can you? Simply talk about something else. Or tell him you'd rather not discuss that subject."

Easier said than done. What did they have to talk about, other than her ruining his life and their physical attraction to each other? How much he resented her? "I did. He kept staring at me through dinner."

"Oh, but that's a positive step forward, Melody! Isn't it? You don't look very happy. Isn't that what you wanted?"

"I wanted him to notice me because of me, not because he disapproves . . ." She bit her bottom lip. "Suffice to say, I'm resigned to the fact he'll never look upon me with affection or approval."

"Oh, but—"

"No, he said he and I will never wed." Remembering how he'd looked when he uttered those words, Melody didn't note the long silence until she looked at Maddy.

"My brother said that to you?"

Melody patted Maddy's hand. "Don't look so shocked. Yes, he did but he has good reason."

"The unfortunate incident you spoke of?"

"That, and other things." So many things. She *had* ruined his life. Of course, ruined her own as well. The wood nymph song had bound them for life, their attraction for each other the only attraction possible. Blunderingly, the girl at sixteen who'd asked a song of love be sung to the man she hoped to wed had a song of lust sung instead. Love, lust, being as one for life was all the same to the wood nymphs. She hadn't known. Not that it mattered at this point, since he didn't believe she hadn't known. Doubtless he'd go to his grave believing she meant to trap him into marriage by way of the wood nymph song of lust. Then, the nasty incident when her family tried to kill him, believing he was forcing himself on her. She shook her head. "No, your brother has very good reason."

* * * *

"Did you see her face when Ardmoor didn't appear?" Maddy asked her husband once alone in their chamber.

"No, my attention wasn't focused on Lady Melody. Although I'm afraid his nonappearance was my fault. I mentioned I saw him speaking to Lady Melody, and apparently I wasn't the only one who'd noticed. Must have spooked him."

Maddy tilted her head. "For the moment, perhaps, for he did enter later. Sadly, it was after Melody retired. I think he came intending to speak to her. I'm sure of it, because he scowled when he didn't see her and it looked as if he mouthed a curse before leaving the room. So!" She laughed and smiled at her husband. "Perhaps it was best it happened the way it did. Now he has to wait until tomorrow. The anticipation will build, you see."

"Then I did a good thing?"

"You always do the correct thing, Robert."

"Then shall you reward me?"

Chapter Seven
Ardmoor Weakens

Last evening, Spode had said how delightful it was to see he and Lady Melody were speaking. His cousin Victor had said Lady Melody was a wonderfully warm woman, and Ardmoor should make haste in wooing her. Mr. Heacock had allowed as how he and his wife were much taken with Lady Melody and how pleased they were to see someone finally appreciated her worth. When a fourth had made reference to how well they looked as a couple, Ardmoor decided against following the men when they joined the ladies in the drawing room and retired to his chamber. The next time he and Melody spoke, it would be away from inquisitive eyes. If not careful, people would begin to imagine he and Melody as a couple. Betrothed.

Now Ardmoor was up, dressed, his wish imbued peg-ribbon tied on securely, and seated in the breakfast room—waiting for Melody. He knew she hadn't gone riding, for he'd sent a note asking if she'd ride with him and she'd agreed. She would expect he'd talk to her then about her foolish, dangerous plan. Instead he planned to speak to her after breakfast. So far he was the only guest in the room, and he assumed the rest were either riding or breakfasting in their chambers. At least he hoped so. He didn't want anyone to see him and Melody together.

Ardmoor rose at her entrance, bid her good morning. Guilt flitted briefly across his mind when he saw her surprise. Had he behaved so boorishly in the past that such elemental proprieties caused her amazement? He went to her, offering to carry her plate. She looked at him, her eyes opened wide, her mouth a perfect 'O'. That mouth, those rosy lips that needed to be kissed. He fought against the compulsion to dash the plate to the floor and sweep her into a close embrace.

Maddy entered and he scowled at her soft laughter. "Good morning," she sang. Now the urge was gone, although who knew when such a desire would return. He jiggled Melody's plate. "I haven't got all morning," he muttered.

She nodded, her face flushed, the sight of which caused him another urge like the one before. Was she feeling need as well? He peered into her face. The answer was yes. Their gazes locked and Ardmoor felt his body heat, his arousal strong. Simultaneously a peace settled over him, a contentment he'd not felt in years—if ever. Yes, she was right about that soul business, she *was* the other half of his soul. He knew Melody felt the same, it radiated from her eyes. Surely he'd never see eyes that shade of grey again. So big and beautiful. And so much to see in them. He wanted to draw her away and spend the next year studying their grey depths. Which estate? The one in Cornwall. Yes, that was the most remote. He wanted to kiss away the tears that suddenly sprang into her lovely eyes. He leaned forward, part of him wondering when he'd cupped her cheek with his hand, when she'd covered it with her own trembling hand. Then Maddy's voice intruded, abruptly pulling him back. He stepped away from Melody.

Bloody hell, what had he . . .?

"Ardmoor, what are you about?" Maddy cried, pushing her way between him and Melody. "This is neither the time nor place for wooing!"

Ardmoor shook his head. How the bloody hell could he talk privately with Melody without . . . His attention was drawn to the footman sweeping up pieces of a broken plate. Apparently he *had* dashed it to the floor. Just as well Maddy had come upon them. No telling what he might have done. Just like before. He groaned, turned, and exited the room.

* * * *

Melody headed toward the drawing room, her appetite gone. Her hopes crushed as well. The state of her heart didn't bear consideration. For a moment she'd been sure Trevor returned her love, but it had just been the wood nymph lust taking hold. She'd seen his expression when his mind cleared, and there'd been no aspect of love present. If Maddy hadn't intruded, what would Trevor have done? Melody bit her lip and shook her head, shame filling her at the realization she'd have welcomed any attention from him. Which would have necessitated a wedding, for which he'd never forgive her. Dore was right, Trevor would never offer for her, so why did she always forget and raise her hopes in that direction only to see them crushed?

Melody halted when Trevor approached. His face grim, his colors indicated turmoil. Doubtless her colors did as well. Was he about to order her to leave?

"Will you join me in Spode's study? He'll act as chaperone. We need to talk, but it's obvious we can't be alone together without another unfortunate incident arising."

Melody swallowed her resentment. Why did he make it sound like something horrible? The incident was unfortunate, yet some of it had been wonderful. Until her family tried to carve out . . . She wouldn't think about that.

"Very well," she replied and followed.

* * * *

"You want me to *what?*" Spode had nearly shouted.

"You heard me," Ardmoor replied. "Just keep your pistol visible and pointed at my peg. If I make a move to rise, remind me, loudly, you'll shoot it off."

"Yes, I heard all that. What I meant was *why* I should do this. I thought the point of the pistol was to make you listen to Lady Melody. I don't understand why you need—"

"You don't have to understand, that's between Lady Melody and myself. Will you do it?"

"I was supposed to help Maddy with the decorations. She's organizing—"

"Just tell my sister I need your presence whilst Lady Melody and I talk. She'll understand."

* * * *

Ardmoor opened Spode's study door for her, met her surprised expression with arched brows. "Spode has agreed to assist in keeping me in my chair. *Away from you. We'll conduct this conversation silently. I trust Spode not to listen. Do you agree?*"

She nodded, smiled at Spode, and then sat. "*You need a pistol?*"

He sat across from her, placing his cane between his legs. "*Apparently so,*" he replied. He frowned at his bow and wondered if his niece's wishes might be the cause of his weakening toward Melody. Because it was obvious he was weakening. He could no longer summon a healthy rage when he thought of the unfortunate incident. He looked up at her. "*Nor will we intrude on each other's private thoughts.*"

"*Agreed.*"

He paused as she straightened her posture, and a flame of irritation blew hot in his belly when she shielded herself against him. Her shield immediately grew stronger. "*Why do you shield against me?*" She winced. He blinked in surprise when he felt it.

"*Why does anyone shield themselves? Protection. Your words wound me. Your thoughts wound me, even when I can't hear them. Your anger wounds me.*"

"*I have never—*"

"*You're not aware of it,*" she replied. "*Why do you think I shield myself? When Dore forces me to attend the Season, I'm—*"

"*In agony,*" Ardmoor finished for her. How had he known that? Yet he had. *His* mind remembered the agony *she'd* felt. "*You're picking up everyone's thoughts, aren't you? Good God, has no one shown you how to shield without encasing your entire body?*"

"*Of course. It doesn't always work.*"

His eyes narrowed when she looked at her hands folded in her lap. Rules and propriety dictated he couldn't enter her mind to see what that meant, but had a feeling if he did, he wouldn't care for the reason. "*Why doesn't it always work?*"

"*You don't want to know.*"

"*Yes, I'd figured that out. Tell me why.*" His heart lurched when he looked into her pain filled eyes. What was wrong with him? Why was he feeling her emotions?

"*I can't function normally unless you're near. It's silly, I daresay a result of the wood nymph song, but unless I completely encase myself I hear and feel everything. It's exhausting.*"

"*Yet my presence somehow allows you to—*"

"*I told you the other night, your presence strengthens me. Since I could function quite normally before the wood nymphs sang to us, and afterward I couldn't, not unless you were near, I believe any reasonable person would conclude your presence is what makes the difference. May we speak of something else?*"

He sat back, his gaze roaming her colors before resting on her face. She spoke true. He didn't need to touch her to discern the truth. How draining for her. Ten years of this? How extraordinarily strong she must be. Was it possible this was the reason for her claim to want to help the magistrates? He could see how it might be a source of relief for her.

"*Did you have a love?*" she asked. "*Did I ruin that for you, too? Was there a woman you thought to woo and wed?*"

Ardmoor waited a moment before replying. "*Before the Unfortunate Incident? No, there was no one.*" Her shield lightened at his reply. "*I believe I understand why you say you want to help the magistrates. But it won't do, you know. I can't allow you to risk your life.*" He couldn't help grinning at her expression. Yes, if eyes could throw daggers he'd be shredded.

"*First off,*" he mused, "*you can't go hunting for particular thoughts, you know that's against the rules. If a murderous thought comes through that clear, then of course you can't ignore it and we're obliged to do something about it. You, however, appear to be an exception. Whether you want them or not, you're picking up everyone's thoughts, even idle ones. That doesn't mean you have to act on them. If you did—*"

"*I have! I picked up on a murderer. He'd not long before committed the crime, so I followed him to his house, saw where he put his knife and the money he'd stolen. Then I alerted the magistrates. He was arrested.*" Melody looked very pleased with herself.

"You followed a murderer to his home?" Ardmoor shouted as he rose.

"I have a gun!" Spode called out.

Ardmoor banged his cane on the floor. "I need to stand." He glared at Melody. *"Just how did you follow him? Bloody hell! A murderer? What were you thinking?"*

"I don't think I care to remain here any longer," Melody said as she rose.

"Of course you don't, because you know what you did was wrong!"

"I can hear you," Spode said.

"How was it wrong?" she cried.

"I can hear you," Spode repeated.

"How was it wrong?"

"*How did you follow him?*" Ardmoor demanded. "*Ha! Just as I thought. Do you know how dangerous using The Shadow is?*"

"*Since that's how I rescued your horse, yes, I have an idea. I know what I'm doing.*"

"*Do you always* think *you know best?*"

"*Yes!*"

"Quiet those thoughts, I can hear you," Spode said softly. "If I can, so can others."

Ardmoor motioned with his hand for Melody to sit and he did the same. "*Do you realize what you did could get you killed? I'm not speaking of just The Shadow. There are people like us who monitor what goes on. And the reason they monitor is to make sure the many people not like us never realize we exist. If they deemed you a threat to our existence, your life would be over before you felt a whisper of their presence. That's a fact.*"

He waited while she processed what he'd said, resisting the urge to pull her onto his lap and comfort her. No! No laps! "*Using The Shadow for travel would get you noticed, too. They're regularly patrolled.*"

"*But I did a good thing! Why should that—*"

"*The one time is fine. But you can wager you were noticed, and they'll be watching to see if you do something like that again.*" When her eyes brimmed with tears his throat constricted. He pushed away her disappointment from him before his chest grew as hot and as tight as hers. The idea of comforting her in his lap returned, the urge quite strong. They did have a chaperone, so surely a little comforting wouldn't be amiss?

"*Then I am doomed.*" She rose and he quickly followed. "*You've had your say, you've warned me.*"

"*You won't pursue this idea?*" He narrowed his eyes when she didn't immediately reply.

"*I suppose gambling hells are monitored?*"

Her shoulders sagged when he nodded. His one brow arched. "*Have you ever been to a gambling hell?*"

"*No, but I enjoy playing cards. It seemed a pleasant way to amass funds so I could be free of Dore.*"

"*By cheating?*"

"*Of course not! No, only those who were already cheating. You know people cheat all the time!*"

"Yes, but it's not up to me or you to administer justice. Cross that idea off your list." She turned away, but not before Ardmoor saw despair envelop her body. He stepped back to keep away, yet at the same time battled against grabbing and holding her close until despair and sadness were cleansed from her. Yes, he was weakening; weakening badly. *"I did want to talk more about the nature of your gifts."*

She stopped, but didn't turn to face him. "Another time perhaps."

"Then later, during our ride." What was he doing? Just because she was sad and he felt the world was coming down on him—courtesy of the bloody wood nymph song that bound him to her and her emotions—didn't mean he had to make her feel better. Except at that moment he could do nothing less than take away her sadness.

Her expression was one of surprise. *"You still want to ride with me?"*

"That's what was agreed upon, wasn't it?" She smiled in response. Yes, he was in deep now, because he really *did* want to ride with her. Her smile warmed his heart, but also sent chills of apprehension down his spine. The more time he spent with her, the more he found to appreciate. The fear, never expressed yet ever present, the fear of rejection because of his peg leg came nipping at his heels, both present and missing. *"Thought you'd like to see how I ride with my peg."*

Her expression turned serious while she searched his eyes. *"I was told you have a special boot,"* she said slowly, as if not sure she should know that bit of information.

Ardmoor breathed a little easier. *"Yes, Watkins made it for me. My peg leg has caused many changes in my life. I doubt most people are aware of the difficulty facing anyone missing a limb."*

She stared intently, a small frown creased her brow. Then her eyes opened wide. *"Oh, but it doesn't—"* She stopped, as if aware of the impropriety if she finished her sentence.

Ardmoor nodded. She understood him. It was enough for now.

* * * *

"There you are!" Maddy said when her husband strolled into the conservatory. She rushed forward and took him aside. "What is your opinion about their meeting? Lady Melody just smiled when I asked how it went, but of course we couldn't talk privately. She appeared happy although her attention wandered as she helped with the decorations. She said she and Ardmoor are going riding. Do you think that wise?"

"I thought you were hoping for a match between them."

"Yes, but I wouldn't want it forced. You didn't see how Ardmoor acted this morning. I thought he'd ravish her in the breakfast room!" At her husband's raised brows she added, "Well, it did look like he was going to kiss her."

"Did Lady Melody protest?"

"No, she appeared quite under his spell. Or he under hers, it was difficult to tell. Much like Wickerdun and..."

Maddy and Spode locked eyes. "Didn't Ardmoor say—"

Spode pressed his finger against her lips. "I don't believe now is the time for speculation, dearest. Too many interested people are near.

"But to ease your mind, Ardmoor and I had a long chat after he and Lady Melody spoke. He is a man on the verge. Of what, I don't think he's yet decided. But I believe the two will be safe. He said Watkins will chaperone them."

* * * *

Melody adjusted her hat and turned her head to see how her plume waved. Her riding costume was all the same shade of azure blue, a color she wore well. Her gloved hands smoothed her skirt until they began trembling.

Would she see Trevor's eyes shine with admiration? Ten years she'd waited for him to evince an interest in her. Was she getting her hopes up only to have them dashed yet again? She held out her hands and tried to steady them. She didn't want to be nervous. Ten years. Was it possible his anger had abated enough he could look at her without seeing the girl who'd ruined his life? Or had she misread his intentions? Ten years. This ride might be her last chance.

And the ride had been his suggestion! He asked *her* to accompany *him*. He didn't want to avoid her, he wanted her company! Good God! She was going riding with Trevor! Sinking onto a chair, she forced back tears. Tears of joy, surely, except . . . she didn't feel joy. More like terror. Suppose he discovered he didn't like her? He liked her ten years ago, but that was . . . ten years ago.

He said he wanted to talk more about her gifts. Was that all this was? Just a friendly conversation? And he'd asked her when she was still reeling from having her future plans failing before she'd even tried. But no, his remarks regarding his peg leg were not idle conversation.

Melody took a deep breath. Another. The only ethical way to find out what his intentions were toward her was to join him. She stood and shook out her skirt. Really, she was acting like a silly school girl. Just because this ride might determine the future course of her life was no reason to sit and plague herself with unanswerable questions.

Another look in the mirror and she smiled. Good. Trevor would approve, she was sure of it. As long as she didn't blurt out anything to give him a disgust of her, there was a chance she might win him over.

Chapter Eight
Ardmoor Comes to a Decision

Ardmoor stood waiting with their horses at the front of the house, recalling his visit here a year ago. Would next Christmas see him here again? Or would he be celebrating on one of his estates with his countess? He didn't know. Absently stroking and patting Presto, he looked at the door as she neared it. She stepped out when the door opened.

His heart leapt at the sight of her. *It bloody well leapt!* There was no escaping her. No escaping the fact they'd be wed before long. No, he should just lie down and grovel at her feet now, tell her to step all over him for the years of hurt he'd caused her. Write to her brother to have the banns called. No escape.

Then she stumbled when she saw him. His arousal grew at the sight of her, grew at the knowledge she desired him as much as he desired her. They were both caught in the lust binding them.

And that's what caught in his craw.

Would he want to wed her, bed her, have her as mother to his children if the *Unfortunate Incident* had never occurred?

Would she still want him if not for the wood nymph lust? Especially since he now had a peg leg?

There was no way of knowing. Absolutely no bloody way of knowing.

He crossed to escort her to their horses. "Will you be warm enough?" Her chagrin shot through him. "You look lovely, by the way. You always do. But today is colder than it has been. Might snow tonight. Will you be warm enough?" Her delight wafted by gently and he bit back a grin.

She smiled and nodded. Then saw his horse. "Oh, you still have . . ."

"Yes, Presto is still with me." He stopped and faced her. "I thank you for saving him. It must have been a frightening experience for you."

"Yes, it was rather unnerving."

He chuckled at the images she released. "You were very brave. And I thank you for your effort, though foiled by me, to save my miserable self as well." Before she could reply they'd reached the horses.

"The boot, as you can see,"—he held it up briefly—"is the other half of the pair. Watkins came up with the idea to buckle my peg inside so I can ride with more stability." By this time he was buckled into the boot. "Watkins will be our chaperone."

"Have you ever considered wearing the boot for other—"

"Yes, I tried, but I can't walk in the bl-blasted thing. May I assist you or would you rather use the block?" Their eyes met, the mutual attraction took over and he backed up. "The mounting block it is. Watkins! Help Lady Melody."

* * * *

It was a pleasure she'd not anticipated. They started out slow until the horses warmed and then they raced. Not as they had ten years ago, but still they raced and laughed for the sheer pleasure of speed and wind in their faces. She lost her hat, but didn't care. It was wonderful.

He talked to her. Spoke as if she hadn't ruined his life. Talked to her like men talked to women they liked. Or courted. That point she couldn't decide upon. No man had ever gotten that far with her—she'd never been inclined to allow familiarity since none had been deemed worthy, for her to make a fair comparison.

He eschewed passing trees when he could, cursing silently when they couldn't be avoided. His *bloody wood nymphs* sounded more like an unthinking habitual response rather than an accusation aimed at her. Therefore she was puzzled when he had them headed for a copse of trees. She saw the cottage and her heart slammed into her chest. What was . . .?

"I thought we'd have a private nuncheon if that's agreeable."

Melody saw Watkins not far behind them. Should she consent?

"Spode said he'd have the kitchen send something."

Ah, so the earl knew about this. She supposed it was all right, then. Except it was *Trevor*. She'd be alone with Trevor. If a repeat of this morning should occur, they'd have to wed, for there would be no Maddy to bring them to their senses. And Trevor would despise her if lust brought him to the altar with her.

"Watkins will be near."

She turned, aware he'd heard every word. She blinked upon realizing she hadn't shielded her thoughts. Why did he flip her wits upside down? Her face heated when he threw back his head and laughed. He was still smiling when he helped her down.

It was the finest meal she'd ever shared. They dined on meat and potato pasties, fruit tarts, nuts and cider. She smiled when it was presented, for it was obviously not a meal planned for seduction. He reminisced about his visit to Spode Hall last Christmas, described how his niece and her wishes completely disrupted long-held plans, and made her laugh when he imitated her cousin Wickerdun.

"He wasn't aware of his gifts at that time," Ardmoor said. "He thought we were all mad when we discussed our wild blood."

Melody frowned. "But at the wedding, he—"

"His wife was able to get through to him and help him remember. She made it a condition of their marriage. His wife has gifts nearly as strong as yours. Do you realize how unusual you are? How talented?"

Melody tucked her head. He'd complimented her!

"More cider? I apologize for the meagerness of the meal, but I didn't think wine would be wise."

She looked up at Trevor and quickly glanced at the table. She wished she could undo everything. She wished they could be like a normal couple. She wished they didn't have to always be aware of the lust . . . She wished she hadn't taken away his choice.

"It's all right, Melody," he said quietly.

She felt tears come to her eyes and shook her head. "No, it isn't all right. I've taken away your choice. I wish—"

"Yes, you took away *our* choice. But what's done is done, my dear. And you know what will follow."

She looked up at him, not liking the resignation in his voice.

"I can offer *you* a choice," he said. "I know some people who could use your gifts. They have plenty of men you see, but every now and then a situation arises where a woman would be more useful than a man. It would be anonymous work, but you'd have the satisfaction of knowing you were helping mankind. Does that interest you?"

It hit her so hard she thought she would fall to the floor. He didn't want to marry her. Not at all. He was trying to find something useful for her to do. Was she so abhorrent he could refuse the pull of their mutual attraction? She wanted to . . .

Then she was in his lap, although he was holding her as far from him as he could. She was so offended, if her arms weren't held by his she'd have struck him.

"Melody, you've veered away from what I was telling you, imagining scenarios that don't exist. I offer you the choice so you won't be forced to wed me, a man with a peg leg. And the reason I hold you at a distance is because of what would happen if I followed my inclination."

"Oh." He didn't hold her in abhorrence. In fact, it sounded like he might like to kiss her. Or would he? She wished she could be sure his desire was true or if it was the wood nymph lust affecting him. "But your leg doesn't matter to me," she hastened to assure him. "Really, it doesn't . . ."

"You say that and I believe you. But if the *Unfortunate Incident* never occurred, would you still feel that way? It's a repugnant sight for a lady to behold."

"You forget my gifts. I have seen it," she snapped. "As for my feeling this way if I'd never asked for the wood nymph song, yes, I believe I would. I've had ten years to think about you, eight Seasons of looking over what was offered in the way of men, and I still choose you." Her eyes narrowed when a smug smile made a brief appearance on his countenance. "Although aware of your faults, well aware of them, I choose you. Tell me plain if you'll have me, for I cannot take much more of being near you without . . ." She stopped and shook her head. "No, forgive me, that was poorly said. But I would know how you feel about me. For if you come to hate me for forcing our marriage, I'd rather not wed at all."

* * * *

Ardmoor blew out a deep breath and pulled her a little closer. This was going to be easier than he dared hope. "That's what I was wondering, my dear. I thought this day would end with our announcing our betrothal. I imagined having to smile and accept congratulations whilst cringing inside." He smiled when she stiffened. "But, my dear Melody, while we were enjoying ourselves, it occurred to me if I were meeting you for the first time I'd consider myself quite fortunate to have you look with favor upon me. I decided I would pursue you. Realized I didn't have to, you were already mine, so to speak. And I further realized if I got around the fact there had been an unfortunate incident, I liked you. I think I always have, which I believe is what so infuriated me. Caused me to act like such a reprehensible fool. Please forgive me."

She smiled, looked deep into his eyes and he knew he'd made the right decision. He pulled her closer and just about spent himself when she licked her lips. He licked his own in anticipation. He was aware the door opened, but ignored the fact since it was only Watkins. She parted her lips and he angled his head. The barrel of a pistol at his ear cooled his ardor.

"Just following orders, my lord," Watkins said.

"I said to threaten my peg, you bloody fool, not my head!"

"I did, my lord, and you ignored me. Thought you'd pay attention if I had it at your temple."

"Right. Put away the pistol. And be the first to congratulate me, Watkins. Lady Melody and I are to marry. Joy will be pleased to know her Christmas wish for me is coming true." He turned to Melody. "My niece wished I might marry so she could have a new aunt."

"Actually, you never asked." She smiled. "But the answer is yes. It would be my honor to be your wife, Trevor."

They rose and held hands. He could feel her joy, knew she could feel his emotions. Could tell when she felt his lust, and felt when it was returned. He laughed. Yes, this marriage would work out very well. And now he could ask the question that had haunted him for ten years. "If you didn't ask the wood nymphs to sing a song of binding lust, what was it you asked them to sing?"

She smiled, brought his hands to her lips and kissed them. "I asked them to sing you a song of my love."

Ardmoor's heart swelled. It bloody well swelled! Yes, this marriage would work out very well.

About the Author

Gerri Bowen loves to read and loves to write. She lives happily in Pennsylvania with her family. If you enjoy her stories, she would like to hear from you at www.gerribowenauthor@gmail.com.

Visit her website at:
http://www.gerribowen.com

Praise for
Highland Press Books!

The Mosquito Tapes - Nobody tells a bio-terror story better than Chris Holmes. Just nobody. And like all of Chris Holmes' books, this one begins well— when San Diego County Chief Medical Examiner Jack Youngblood discovers a strange mosquito in the pocket of a murder victim. Taut, tingly, and downright scary, *The Mosquito Tapes* will keep you reading well into the night. But best be wary: Spray yourself with Deet and have a fly swatter nearby.
~ *Ben F. Small, author of Alibi On Ice and The Olive Horseshoe, a Preditors & Editors Top Ten Pick*

* * * *

Cynthia Breeding's **Prelude to Camelot** is a lovely and fascinating read, a book worthy of being shelved with my Arthurania fiction and non-fiction.
~ *Brenda Thatcher, Mystique Books*

* * * *

Romance on Route 66 by Judith Leigh and Cheryl Norman – Norman and Leigh break the romance speed limit on America's historic roadway.
~ *Anne Krist, Ecataromance Reviewers' Choice Award Winner*

* * * *

Ah, the memories that **Operation: L.O.V.E.** brings to mind. As an Air Force nurse who married an Air Force fighter pilot, I relived the days of glory through each and every story. While covering all the military branches, each story holds a special spark of its own that readers will love!
~ *Lori Avocato, Best Selling Author*

* * * *

In **Fate of Camelot**, Cynthia Breeding develops the Arthur-Lancelot-Gwenhwyfar relationship. In many Arthurian tales, Guinevere is a rather flat character. Cynthia Breeding gives her a depth of character as the reader sees her love for Lancelot and her devotion to the realm as its queen. The reader feels the pull she experiences between both men. In addition, the reader feels more of the deep friendship between Arthur and Lancelot seen in Malory's Arthurian tales. In this area, Cynthia Breeding is more faithful to the medieval Arthurian tradition than a glamorized Hollywood version. She does not gloss over the difficulties of Gwenhwyfar's role as queen and as woman, but rather develops them to give the reader a vision of a woman who lives her role as queen and lover with all that she is.

~ Merri, Merrimon Books

* * * *

Rape of the Soul - Ms. Thompson's characters are unforgettable. Deep, promising and suspenseful this story was. I couldn't put it down. Around every corner was something that you didn't know was going to happen. If you love a sense of history in a book, then I suggest reading this book!
~ Ruth Schaller, Paranormal Romance Reviews

* * * *

Static Resistance and Rose – An enticing, fresh voice. Lee Roland knows how to capture your heart.
~ Kelley St. John, National Readers Choice Award Winner

* * * *

Southern Fried Trouble - Katherine Deauxville is at the top of her form with mayhem, sizzle and murder.
~ Nan Ryan, NY Times Best-Selling Author

* * * *

Madrigal: A Novel of Gaston Leroux's Phantom of the Opera takes place four years after the events of the original novel. The classic novel aside, this book is a wonderful historical tale of life, love, and choices. However, the most impressive aspect that stands out to me is the writing. Ms. Linforth's prose is phenomenally beautiful and hauntingly breathtaking.
~ Bonnie-Lass, Coffee Time Romance

* * * *

Cave of Terror by Amber Dawn Bell - Highly entertaining and fun, ***Cave of Terror*** was impossible to put down. Though at times dark and evil, Ms. Bell never failed to inject some light-hearted humor into the story. Delightfully funny with a true sense of teenagers, Cheyenne is believable and her emotional struggles are on par with most teens. The author gave just enough background to understand the workings of her vampires. I truly enjoyed Ryan and Constantine. Ryan was adorable and a teenager's dream. Constantine was deliciously dark. Ms. Bell has done an admirable job of telling a story suitable for young adults.
~ Dawnie, Fallen Angel Reviews

* * * *

The Sense of Honor - Ashley Kath-Bilsky has written a historical romance of the highest caliber. This reviewer fell in love with the hero and was cheering for the heroine all the way through. The plot is exciting, characters are multi-dimensional, and the secondary characters bring life to the story. Sexual tension rages through this story and Ms. Kath-Bilsky gives her readers a breathtaking romance. The love scenes are sensual and very romantic. This reviewer was very pleased with how the author handled all the secrets and both characters reacted very maturely when the secrets finally came to light.
~ Valerie, Love Romances and More

* * * *

Highland Wishes by Leanne Burroughs. The storyline, set in a time when tension was high between England and Scotland, is a fast-paced tale. The reader can feel this author's love for Scotland and its many wonderful heroes. This reviewer was easily captivated by the story and was enthralled by it until the end. The reader will laugh and cry as you read this wonderful story. The reader feels all the pain, torment and disillusionment felt by both main characters, but also the joy and love they felt. Ms. Burroughs has crafted a well-researched story that gives a glimpse into Scotland during a time when there was upheaval and war for independence. This reviewer commends her for a wonderful job done.

~*Dawn Roberto, Love Romances*

* * * *

I adore this Scottish historical romance! *Blood on the Tartan* has more history than some historical romances—but never dry history! Readers will find themselves completely immersed in the scene, the history and the characters. Chris Holmes creates a multi-dimensional theme of justice in his depiction of all the nuances and forces at work from the laird down to the land tenants. This intricate historical detail emanates from the story itself, heightening the suspense and the reader's understanding of the history in a vivid manner as if it were current and present. The extra historical detail just makes their life stories more memorable and lasting because the emotions were grounded in events. *Blood On The Tartan* is a must read for romance and historical fiction lovers of Scottish heritage.

~Merri, *Merrimon Reviews*

* * * *

Chasing Byron by Molly Zenk is a page turner of a book not only because of the engaging characters, but also by the lovely prose. Reading this book was a jolly fun time all through the eyes of Miss Woodhouse, yet also one that touches the heart. It was an experience I would definitely repeat. Ms. Zenk must have had a glorious time penning this story.

~*Orange Blossom, Long and Short Reviews*

* * * *

Moon of the Falling Leaves is an incredible read. The characters are not only believable, but the blending in of how Swift Eagle shows Jessica and her children the acts of survival is remarkably done. Diane Davis White pens a poignant tale that really grabbed this reader. She tells a descriptive story of discipline, trust and love in a time where hatred and prejudice abounded among many. This rich tale offers vivid imagery of the beautiful scenery and landscape, and brings in the tribal customs of each person, as Jessica and Swift Eagle search their heart.

~*Cherokee, Coffee Time Romance*

* * * *

Jean Harrington's *The Barefoot Queen* is a superb historical with a lushly painted setting. I adored Grace for her courage and the cleverness with which she sets out to make Owen see her love for him. The bond between Grace and Owen is tenderly portrayed and their love had me rooting for them right up until the last page. Ms. Harrington's *The Barefoot Queen* is a treasure in the historical romance genre you'll want to read for yourself!

Five Star Pick of the Week!!!

~ Crave More Romance

* * * *

Almost Taken by Isabel Mere takes the reader on an exciting adventure. The compelling characters of Deran Morissey, the Earl of Atherton, and Ava Fychon, a young woman from Wales, find themselves drawn together as they search for her missing siblings.
This is a sensual romance, and a creative and fast moving storyline that will enthrall readers. Ava, who is highly spirited and stubborn, will win the respect of the readers for her courage and determination. Deran, who is rumored in the beginning to be an ice king, not caring about anyone, will prove how wrong people's perceptions can be. **Almost Taken** is an emotionally moving historical romance that I highly recommend.

~ Anita, The Romance Studio

* * * *

Leanne Burroughs easily will captivate the reader with intricate details, a mystery that ensnares the reader and characters that will touch their hearts. By the end of the first chapter, this reviewer was enthralled with **Her Highland Rogue** and was rooting for Duncan and Catherine to admit their love. Laughter, tears and love shine through this wonderful novel. This reviewer was amazed at Ms. Burroughs' depth and perception in this storyline. Her wonderful way with words plays itself through each page like a lyrical note and will captivate the reader till the very end.
Read **Her Highland Rogue** and be transported to a time full of mystery and promise of a future. This reviewer is highly recommending this book for those who enjoy an engrossing Scottish tale full of humor, love and laughter.

~Dawn Roberto, Love Romances

* * * *

Bride of Blackbeard by Brynn Chapman is a compelling tale of sorrow, pain, love, and hate. From the moment I started reading about Constanza and her upbringing, I was torn. Each of the people she encounters on her journey has an experience to share, drawing in the reader more. Ms. Chapman sketches a story that tugs at the heartstrings. I believe many will be touched in some way by this extraordinary book that leaves much thought.

~ Cherokee, Coffee Time Romance

* * * *

Isabel Mere's skill with words and the turn of a phrase makes **Almost Guilty** a joy to read. Her characters reach out and pull the reader into the trials, tribulations, simple pleasures, and sensual joy that they enjoy.
Ms. Mere unravels the tangled web of murder, smuggling, kidnapping, hatred and faithless friends, while weaving a web of caring, sensual love that leaves a special joy and hope in the reader's heart.

~ Camellia, Long and Short Reviews

* * * *

Beats A Wild Heart - In the ancient, Celtic land of Cornwall, Emma Hayward searched for a myth and found truth. The legend of the black cat of Bodmin Moor is a well known Cornish legend. Jean Adams has merged the essence of myth and romance into a fascinating story which catches the imagination. I enjoyed the way the story unfolded at a smooth and steady pace with Emma and Seth appearing as real people who feel an instant attraction for one another. At first the story appears to be straightforward, but as it evolves mystery, love and intrigue intervene to make a vibrant story with hidden depths. ***Beats a Wild Heart*** is well written and a pleasure to read. Once you start reading you won't be able to put this book down.

~ *Orchid, Long and Short Reviews*

* * * *

***Down Home Ever Lovin' Mule* Blues** by Jacquie Rogers - How can true love fail when everyone and their mule, cat, and skunk know that Brody and Rita belong together, even if Rita is engaged to another man?
Needless to say, this is a fabulous roll on the floor while laughing out loud story. I am so thrilled to discover this book, and the author who wrote it. Rarely do I locate a story with as much humor, joy, and downright lust spread so thickly on the pages that I am surprised I could turn the pages. ***Down Home Ever Lovin' Mule Blues*** is a treasure not to be missed.

~*Suziq2, Single Titles.com*

* * * *

Saving Tampa - What if you knew something horrible was going to happen but you could prevent it? Would you tell someone? What if you saw it in a vision and had no proof? Would you risk your credibility to come forward? These are the questions at the heart of ***Saving Tampa***, an on-the-edge-of-your-seat thriller from Jo Webnar, who has written a wonderful suspense that is as timely as it is entertaining.

~ *Mairead Walpole, Reviews by Crystal*

* * * *

When the Vow Breaks by Judith Leigh - This book is about a woman who fights breast cancer. I assumed it would be extremely emotional and hard to read, but it was not. The storyline dealt more with the commitment between a man and a woman, with a true belief of God.
The intrigue was that of finding a rock to lean upon through faith in God. Not only did she learn to lean on her relationship with Him, but she also learned how to forgive her husband. This is a great look at not only a breast cancer survivor, but also a couple whose commitment to each other through their faith grew stronger. It is an easy read and one I highly recommend.

~ *Brenda Talley, The Romance Studio*

* * * *

A Heated Romance by Candace Gold - A fascinating romantic suspense tells the story of Marcie O'Dwyer, a female firefighter who has had to struggle to prove herself. While the first part of the book focuses on the romance and Marcie's daily life, the second part transitions into a suspense novel as Marcie witnesses something suspicious at one of the fires. Her life is endangered by what she possibly knows and I found myself anticipating the outcome almost as much as Marcie.

~ *Lilac, Long and Short Reviews*

* * * *

Into the Woods by R.R. Smythe - This Young Adult Fantasy will send chills down your spine. I, as the reader, followed Callum and witnessed everything he and his friends went through as they attempted to decipher the messages. At the same time, I watched Callum's mother, Ellsbeth, as she walked through the Netherwood. Each time Callum deciphered one of the four messages, some villagers awakened. Through the eyes of Ellsbeth, I saw the other sleepers wander, make mistakes, and be released from the Netherwood, leaving Ellsbeth alone. Excellent reading for any age of fantasy fans!

~ *Detra Fitch, Huntress Reviews*

* * * *

Like the Lion, the Witch, and the Wardrobe, ***Dark Well of Decision*** is a grand adventure with a likable girl who is a little like all of us. Zoe's insecurities are realistically drawn and her struggle with both her faith and the new direction her life will take is poignant. The references to the Bible and the teachings presented are appropriately captured. Author Anne Kimberly is an author to watch; her gift for penning a grand childhood adventure is a great one. This one is well worth the time and money spent.

~*Lettetia, Coffee Time Romance*

* * * *

The Crystal Heart by Katherine Deauxville brims with ribald humor and authentic historical detail. Enjoy!

~ *Virginia Henley, NY Times bestselling author*

* * * *

In Sunshine or In Shadow - If you adore the stormy heroes of 'Wuthering Heights' and 'Jane Eyre' (and who doesn't?) you'll be entranced by Cynthia Owens' passionate story of Ireland after the Great Famine, and David Burke - a man from America with a hidden past and a secret name. Only one woman, the fiery, luscious Siobhan, can unlock the bonds that imprison him. Highly recommended for those who love classic romance and an action-packed story.

~ *Best Selling Author, Maggie Davis,*
AKA Katherine Deauxville

* * * *

Rebel Heart - Jannine Corti Petska used a myriad of emotions to tell this story and the reader quickly becomes entranced in the ways Courtney's stubborn attitude works to her advantage in surviving this disastrous beginning to her new life. This is a wonderful rendition of a different type which is a welcome addition to the historical romance genre. I believe you will enjoy this story; I know I did!

~ *Brenda Talley, The Romance Studio*

* * * *

Pretend I'm Yours by Phyllis Campbell is an exceptional masterpiece. This lovely story is so rich in detail and personalities that it just leaps out and grabs hold of the reader. Ms. Campbell carries the reader into a mirage of mystery with deceit, betrayal of the worst kind, and a passionate love that makes this a whirlwind page-turner. This extraordinary read had me mesmerized with its ambiance, its characters and its remarkable twists and turns, making it one recommended read in my book.

~ *Linda L., Fallen Angel Reviews*

* * * *

Cat O' Nine Tales by Deborah MacGillivray. Enchanting tales from the most wicked, award-winning author today. Spellbinding! A treat for all.

~ *Detra Fitch, The Huntress Reviews*

* * * *

Brides of the West by Michèle Ann Young, Kimberly Ivey, and Billie Warren Chai - All three of the stories in this wonderful anthology are based on women who gambled their future in blindly accepting complete strangers for husbands. It was a different era when a woman must have a husband to survive and all three of these phenomenal authors wrote exceptional stories featuring fascinating and gutsy heroines and the men who loved them. For an engrossing read with splendid original stories I highly encourage readers to pick up a copy of this marvelous anthology.

~ *Marilyn Rondeau, Reviewers International Organization*

* * * *

Faery Special Romances - Brilliantly magical! Jacquie Rogers' special brand of humor and imagination will have you believing in faeries from page one. Absolutely enchanting!

~ *Dawn Thompson, Award Winning Author*

* * * *

Flames of Gold *(Anthology)* - Within every heart lies a flame of hope, a dream of true love, a glimmering thought that the goodness of life is far, far larger than the challenges and adversities arriving in every life. In ***Flames of Gold*** lie five short stories wrapping credible characters into that mysterious, poignant mixture of pain and pleasure, sorrow and joy, stony apathy and resurrected hope.

Deftly plotted, paced precisely to hold interest and delightfully unfolding, ***Flames of Gold*** deserves to be enjoyed in any season, guaranteeing that real holiday spirit endures within the gifts of faith, hope and love personified in these engaging, spirited stories!

~ *Viviane Crystal, Reviews by Crystal*

* * * *

Romance Upon A Midnight Clear *(Anthology)* - Each of these stories is well-written; when grouped together, they pack a powerful punch. Each author shares exceptional characters and a multitude of emotions ranging from grief to elation. You cannot help being able to relate to these stories that touch your heart and will entertain you at any time of year, not just the holidays. I feel honored to have been able to sample the works of such talented authors.

~*Matilda, Coffee Time Romance*

* * * *

Christmas is a magical time and twelve talented authors answer the question of what happens when **Christmas Wishes** come true in this incredible anthology. Each of these highly skilled authors brings a slightly different perspective to the Christmas theme to create a book that is sure to leave readers satisfied. What a joy to read such splendid stories! This reviewer looks forward to more anthologies by Highland Press as the quality is simply astonishing.

~ *Debbie, CK2S Kwips and Kritiques*

* * * *

Recipe for Love (Anthology) - I don't think the reader will find a better compilation of mouth watering short romantic love stories than in **Recipe for Love**! This is a highly recommended volume—perfect for beaches, doctor's offices, or anywhere you've a few minutes to read.

~ *Marilyn Rondeau, Reviewers International Organization*

* * * *

Holiday in the Heart (Anthology) - Twelve stories that would put even Scrooge into the Christmas spirit. It does not matter what *type* of romance genre you prefer. This book has a little bit of everything. The stories are set in the U.S.A. and Europe. Some take place in the past, some in the present, and one story takes place in both! I strongly suggest you put on something comfortable, brew up something hot (tea, coffee or cocoa will do), light up a fire, settle down somewhere quiet and begin reading this anthology.

~ *Detra Fitch, Huntress Reviews*

* * * *

Blue Moon Magic is an enchanting collection of short stories. **Blue Moon Magic** offers historicals, contemporaries, time travel, paranormal, and futuristic narratives to tempt your heart.

Legend says that if you wish with all your heart upon the rare blue moon, your wishes were sure to come true. In some of the stories, love happens in the most unusual ways. Angels may help, ancient spells may be broken, anything can happen. Even vampires will find their perfect mate with the power of the blue moon.

Blue Moon Magic is a perfect read for late at night or even during your commute to work. The short yet sweet stories are a wonderful way to spend a few minutes. If you do not have the time to finish a full-length novel, and hate stopping in the middle of a loving tale, I highly recommend grabbing this book.

~ *Kim Swiderski, Writers Unlimited Reviewer*

* * * *

Legend has it that a blue moon is enchanted. What happens when fifteen talented authors utilize this theme to create enthralling stories of love?

Readers will find a wide variety of time periods and styles showcased in this superb anthology. **Blue Moon Enchantment** is sure to offer a little bit of something for everyone!

~ Debbie, CK²S Kwips and Kritiques

* * * *

Love Under the Mistletoe is a fun anthology that infuses the beauty of the season with fun characters and unforgettable situations. This is one of those books you can read year round and still derive great pleasure from each of the charming stories. A wonderful compilation of holiday stories.

~ Chrissy Dionne, Romance Junkies

* * * *

Love and Silver Bells - I really enjoyed this heart-warming anthology. The characters are heart-wrenchingly human and hurting and simply looking for a little bit of peace on earth. Luckily they all eventually find it, although not without some strife. But we always appreciate the gifts we receive when we have to work a little harder to keep them. I recommend these warm holiday tales be read by the light of a well-lit tree, with a lovely fire in the fireplace and a nice cup of hot cocoa. All will warm you through and through.

~ Angi, Night Owl Romance

* * * *

Love on a Harley is an amazing romantic anthology featuring six amazing stories. Each story was heartwarming, tear jerking, and so perfect. I got tied to each one wanting them to continue on forever. Lost love, rekindling love, and learning to love are all expressed within these pages beautifully. I couldn't ask for a better romance anthology; each author brings that sensual, longing sort of love that every woman dreams of. Great job ladies!

~ Crystal, Crystal Book Reviews

* * * *

No Law Against Love *(Anthology)* - If you have ever found yourself rolling your eyes at some of the more stupid laws, then you are going to adore this novel. Twenty-four stories fill this anthology, each dealing with at least one stupid or outdated law. Let me give you an example: In Florida, USA, there is a law that states 'If an elephant is left tied to a parking meter, the parking fee has to be paid just as it would for a vehicle.' Yes, you read that correctly. No matter how many times you go back and reread them, the words will remain the same. The tales take place in the present, in the past, in the USA, in England . . . in other words, there is something for everyone! Best yet, profits from the sales of this novel will go to breast cancer prevention.
A stellar anthology that had me laughing, sighing in pleasure, believing in magic, and left me begging for more! This is one novel that will go directly to my 'Keeper' shelf, to be read over and over again. Very highly recommended!

~ Detra Fitch, Huntress Reviews

* * * *

No Law Against Love 2 - I'm sure you've heard about some of those silly laws, right? Well, this anthology shows us that sometimes those silly laws can bring just the right people together.
I highly recommend this anthology. Each story is a gem and each author has

certainly given their readers value for money.

~ Valerie, Love Romances and More

Now Available from Highland Press Publishing:

Non-Fiction/ Writer's Resource:

Rebecca Andrews
The Millennium Phrase Book

Historicals:

Jean Adams
Eternal Hearts

Isabel Mere
Almost Silenced

Jean Harrington
In the Lion's Mouth

Cynthia Breeding
Prelude to Camelot

Cynthia Breeding
Fate of Camelot

Ashley Kath-Bilsky
The Sense of Honor

Isabel Mere
Almost Taken

Isabel Mere
Almost Guilty

Leanne Burroughs
Highland Wishes

Leanne Burroughs
Her Highland Rogue

Chris Holmes
Blood on the Tartan

Jean Harrington
The Barefoot Queen

Linda Bilodeau
The Wine Seekers

Judith Leigh
When the Vow Breaks

Jennifer Linforth

Madrigal
Brynn Chapman
Bride of Blackbeard
Diane Davis White
Moon of the Falling Leaves
Molly Zenk
Chasing Byron
Katherine Deauxville
The Crystal Heart
Cynthia Owens
In Sunshine or In Shadow
Jannine Corti Petska
Rebel Heart
Jeanmarie Hamilton
Seduction
Phyllis Campbell
Pretend I'm Yours
Historical/Horror:
Dawn Thompson
Rape of the Soul
Mystery/Comedic:
Katherine Deauxville
Southern Fried Trouble
Action/Suspense:
Chris Holmes
The Mosquito Tapes
Eric Fullilove
The Zero Day Event
Romantic Suspense:
Candace Gold
A Heated Romance
Jo Webnar
Saving Tampa
Lee Roland
Static Resistance and Rose
Contemporary:
Jean Adams

Beats a Wild Heart
Jacquie Rogers
Down Home Ever Lovin' Mule Blues
Teryl Oswald
Luck of the Draw
Young Adult:
Amber Dawn Bell
Cave of Terror
R.R. Smythe
Into the Woods
Anne Kimberly
Dark Well of Decision
Anthologies:
Anne Elizabeth/Tara Nina/DC DeVane/
Leslie Wainger/Chryssa Carson
For Your Heart Only
Gerri Bowen
Just A Little Wild
Cynthia Breeding/Kirsten Scott/Karen Michelle Nutt/Gerri
Bowen/Erin Hatton/Kimberly Ivey
Second Time Around
Judith Leigh/Cheryl Norman
Romance on Route 66
Anne Elizabeth/C.H. Admirand/DC DeVane/
Tara Nina/Lindsay Downs
Operation: L.O.V.E.
Cynthia Breeding/Kristi Ahlers/Gerri Bowen/
Susan Flanders/ Erin E.M. Hatton
A Dance of Manners
Deborah MacGillivray
Cat O'Nine Tales
Deborah MacGillivray/Rebecca Andrews/
Billie Warren-Chai/Debi Farr/Patricia Frank/
Diane Davis-White
Love on a Harley
Zoe Archer/Amber Dawn Bell/Gerri Bowen/
Candace Gold/Patty Howell/

Kimberly Ivey/Lee Roland
No Law Against Love 2
Michèle Ann Young/Kimberly Ivey/
Billie Warren Chai
Brides of the West
Jacquie Rogers
Faery Special Romances
Holiday Romance Anthology
Christmas Wishes
Holiday Romance Anthology
Holiday in the Heart
Romance Anthology
No Law Against Love
Romance Anthology
Blue Moon Magic
Romance Anthology
Blue Moon Enchantment
Romance Anthology
Recipe for Love
Deborah MacGillivray/Leanne Burroughs/
Amy Blizzard/Gerri Bowen/Judith Leigh
Love Under the Mistletoe
Deborah MacGillivray/Leanne Burroughs/
Rebecca Andrews/Amber Dawn Bell/Erin E.M.
Hatton/Patty Howell/Isabel Mere
Romance Upon A Midnight Clear
Leanne Burroughs/Amber Dawn Bell/Amy Blizzard/
Patty Howell/Judith Leigh
Flames of Gold
Polly McCrillis/Rebecca Andrews/
Billie Warren Chai/Diane Davis White
Love and Silver Bells
Children's Illustrated:
Lance Martin
The Little Hermit
Check our website frequently for
future releases.

www.highlandpress.org

Highland Press

Anthologies

☐ 978-0-9823615-0-4   **Operation: L.O.V.E.**   **$11.99**
☐ 978-0-9823615-2-8   **A Dance of Manners**   **$11.99**
☐ 978-0-9787139-3-5   **Recipe for Love**   **$12.99**

Highland Press Publishing
PO Box 2292, High Springs, FL 32655
www.highlandpress.org

Please send me the books I have checked above. I am enclosing $_____(Please add $2.50 per book to cover shipping and handling). Send check or money order—no C.O.D.s please. Or, PayPal – Leanne@leanneburroughs.com and indicate names of book(s) ordered.

Name_____

Address_____
City_____State/Zip_____

Please allow 2 weeks for delivery. Offer good in US only. (Contact The.Highland.Press@gmail.com for shipping charges outside the US.)